Women's Guide to Navigating Midlife

Dr. Pratiksha Prashant

ISBN 978-93-6263-452-8
Copyright © Dr. Pratiksha Prashant, 2025

First published in India 2025 by Leadstart Inkstate
A brand of One Point Six Technologies Pvt. Ltd.

Unit no. 26, Ground Floor, A1, Shram Safalya,
Wadala Truck Terminal Road, Near Post Office,
Antop Hill, Mumbai - 400037.
Phone: +91 96999 33000
Email: info@leadstartcorp.com
www.leadstartcorp.com

All rights reserved. No part of this publication may be reproduced, distributed, or transmitted in any form or by any means, including photocopying, recording, machine learning, AI, or other electronic or mechanical methods, without the prior written consent of the publisher, except in the case of brief quotation embodied in critical reviews and various other non-commercial uses permitted by copyright law. The resemblance to actual persons, things, living or dead locales, or events is entirely coincidental.

Disclaimer: The views expressed in this book are those of the Author and do not pertain to be held by the Publisher. This is a work of fiction. All characters, names, places, and incidents portrayed in this book are either the product of the author's imagination or are used fictitiously. Any resemblance to actual persons, living or dead, events, or locations is entirely coincidental

Editor: Roona Ballachanda
Cover: Darshil B. Gohel
Layouts: Varad Graphics

About the Author

Dr. Pratiksha Prashant is a health coach and mentor specialising in the wellness of middle-aged women. Her journey in health and wellness began over 25 years ago as a dental surgeon. However, personal and family health struggles motivated her to explore the field of holistic health. This fascination inspired her to complete double majors in health science and nutrition.

A significant turning point in her life occurred in her late thirties when she experienced her own health transition and witnessed the struggles of others. As a result, she decided to focus exclusively on coaching women in health and wellness, becoming an internationally certified health coach from the Institute for Integrative Nutrition (IIN) in New York and acquiring multiple diplomas from prestigious universities.

Now, Dr. Pratiksha offers courses and personal consultations to empower women on their health and wellness journeys. Her husband, Prashant Chandrasekharan, serves in the defense forces, which has inspired her to embrace her wanderlust. Meanwhile, her teenage son, Shreyas, keeps her grounded and connected to her roots.

Acknowledgements

This book is based on my experiences in life, both good and bad. I am deeply grateful to all my loved ones and acquaintances who have shaped my life and this book. To my parents, thank you for providing me with a wonderful childhood filled with countless stories to share with my readers as an author. To my dear husband, thank you for taking me on a lifelong journey of adventure, never allowing me to settle, and being more than just a husband—you have pushed me on my adventure as a first-time author. To my darling son, my first editor and critic, I am grateful for the unconditional love and happiness you have brought into my life and for your patience while reading my early, long, and tedious chapter drafts. To my sisters, thank you for helping me experience a spectrum of emotions that resonate throughout this book.

To my extended family, thank you for embracing me as one of your own, along with all those who have touched my life—kindly and unkindly—teaching me valuable lessons to share. I would also like to extend my gratitude to all the editors of my book, both professional and amateur. A special thank you to Roona, my editor, for providing direction to my book and for never asking me to change its tone. Thank you, Varsha, for introducing me to the nuances of being an author. I am also deeply thankful to my sister, Dr. Suvidha, for her kindness and encouragement, which illuminated this book during my darker days as an author. Thank you, Vrinda, Rajkumari and Mrs Jayati for believing in my work and sharing your insights on my first draft. Lastly, I would like to thank the universe for giving me skills, life lessons, and education and for placing me in the right place at the right time to conceive this book.

Contents

Preface   9

Part 1: Navigating Emotions   13
- Introduction   15
- Envy The Green-Eyed Monster   18
- I Am Not Alone, but Lonely   24
- Whispering of the Soul Depression and Mood Swings   30
- Banishing Boredom   37
- Repressed Anger   40
- Letting Go of Guilt   45
- Regret   51
- Attachment or Detachment   55
- Overcoming Fear   63
- Acknowledging Grief   70

Part 2: Evolving Relationships   77
- Introduction   79
- Made in Heaven - Marriages   81
- Friends   103
- Children   112
- Ageing Parents   131
- Siblings and Extended Family   142

Part 3: Rediscovering Yourself   151
- Introduction   153
- Discovering Your Identity   155
- Setting Boundaries   165
- Forgiving and Healing   172
- Going Back to Faith   178
- Finding Your Passion   184
- Finding Your Purpose   190

Part 4: Redefining Beauty   197
- Introduction   199
- Pot Bellies and Added Kilos   201
- Stories on Your Face: Fine Lines and Wrinkles   218
- Once-Luscious Locks   229

Part 5: Health   241

1. Bone and Cardiovascular Health   243
   - Bone Health   245
   - Cardiovascular Health   252

2. Nourishing Nutrition   264
   - Carbohydrates: Vices and Virtues   266
   - Protein Power   271
   - Omega-3 Fatty Acids   285
   - Fibre   290

3. Addiction to Deaddiction   297
   - Navigating Alcohol   297
   - Highs and Lows of Caffeine   303
   - Smoking Away Life   309

Conclusion   **316**

PREFACE

Somewhere around forty, I was struck by a question that gnawed at my soul: What is my purpose on this earth? Was it my hormones whispering this existential query? Was it the sudden abundance of time as my son found his path? Or was it the stark reality of mortality made evident by my ageing parents?

I was born into a household where education and family were sacred, so I was given the finest schooling. Marriage redirected my focus to my family, and I lost sight of myself in my quest to be the perfect mother and wife. Despite my qualifications, I juggled sporadic jobs with no consistent career growth, but it wasn't until I was forty that the genuine upheaval began. I felt a profound loss of identity, and in my search for answers, I pointed fingers at myself and others, desperately trying to understand the void in my life. An overwhelming sense of purposelessness crept in, striking a blow to my self-esteem. I no longer felt indispensable to my family, and the solace I sought in work escaped me. Even my reflection in the mirror was unfamiliar. Something had changed.

However, a significant shift occurred when I attended my 25th school reunion. It revealed that I was not alone in facing these challenges in life, which sparked a journey of self-discovery.

Initially, I hesitated to attend the reunion, burdened by my emotions. However, the reluctance faded when someone unexpectedly added me to the 25th reunion social group. Suddenly, a wave of excitement swept through me. As the event approached, a palpable buzz of anticipation enveloped us all. Old friends eagerly anticipated reuniting, sparking a flurry of activity – they delicately chose dresses, experimented with makeup, and meticulously selected the perfect venue. Everyone was putting their best foot forward, eager to display their flawless facades.

At the reunion, it initially seemed as if everyone had it all together—ideal partners, successful careers, and happy families. But as the night passed and spirits lifted, the truth behind the polished exteriors emerged. Underneath the mask of perfection, a different reality was unfolding. The layers of superficiality began to peel away, revealing a seething undercurrent of unspoken struggles and hidden vulnerabilities. Despite the outward appearances of contentment—it became evident that we all carried the weight of midlife struggles. This realisation that we are not alone in our battles is a powerful testament to the shared experiences of women in midlife.

Amidst the laughter and pleasantries, the unspoken truth emerged—health issues, family turmoil, and career setbacks silently plagued us all. As the veil of polished perfection gradually lifted, it exposed our experiences of grief over lost loved ones, regrets over paths not taken, and the unrelenting ache of unfulfilled dreams. Emotions ran high as conversations delved into the raw, unvarnished truths of our journey through midlife.

As the night wore on, a sense of resilience emerged from the struggles and quiet resolve of those present. Despite the pains of ageing and the weight of unmet expectations, a glimmer of hope shone through the darkness. Beneath the surface of midlife blues, a longing for a higher purpose united us, transcending the boundaries of our diverse backgrounds and life circumstances.

As I returned from that reunion, my heart felt heavy with mixed emotions that seemed to tug at my very core. Amidst the laughter and reminiscing, a deep sense of gratitude emerged, binding us to the silent understanding of life's universal truths. Realising that time had subtly etched its mark on our once-youthful faces struck a chord within me. The weight of responsibilities, once so burdensome, now seemed to lighten as our children grew older, leaving us with moments of contemplation and aching nostalgia for the bygone days.

I felt a deep sense of introspection wash over me. I realized that this phase of life was not just about surviving but embracing the new—with all its imperfections, vulnerabilities, and hidden longings. Midlife is a time of growth and self-discovery, embracing the changes and finding new paths.

This book is a tribute to all women in midlife, regardless of their marital status, career, or wealth. As

I navigate this transition myself, alongside countless women around me, I realise midlife is when a woman needs to think about herself more than ever because the next phase of life has just begun. This book serves as a heartfelt letter to all middle-aged women, offering support, understanding, and guidance through this transformative period of life. It provides a safe space for women to explore, navigate and make sense of the feelings, emotions, physical transformations and changes in relationships they encounter on this journey. Trust this process, as within it lies the potential to hear your inner voice's whispers clearly amid the storm.

Part One
Navigating Emotions

INTRODUCTION

"Emotions are the colours of the soul; they are spectacular and incredible. When you don't feel, the world becomes dull and colourless."

— **William Paul Young**

During midlife, women are often deeply immersed in the demands of daily life, juggling responsibilities and expectations. Emotions are carefully tucked away in the recesses of their hearts, rarely seeing the light of day. The fear of judgment, of being perceived as weak or overly sensitive, has taught them to master the art of concealment. Over the years, they have become so adept at hiding their negative emotions that they almost become invisible, blending seamlessly with an outwardly calm and composed demeanour. Yet, beneath this facade lies a universal truth: as humans, we cannot escape our emotions. They are an intrinsic part of us, constantly shaping our experiences and perceptions. Occasionally, these emotions break through the surface when our patience reaches its limit. A sharp remark or a sudden, uncharacteristic outburst reveals the pent-up frustration we have been concealing. These moments are not deliberate admissions of our inner struggles but spontaneous eruptions of the stress and discontent we have diligently suppressed. Have you ever felt the weight of unspoken emotions breaking through in unexpected ways?

In today's world, expressing emotions can sometimes feel like wearing a neon sign that says, "I'm vulnerable!" But think about it. What would separate us from our animal friends if we stripped away emotions? Sure, we'd still have our smarts, but emotions? They're like the seasoning that makes life's bland moments more flavourful. Love and happiness get all the airtime because, let's face it, they are the superstars of emotions. But what about those unsung heroes? The ones we keep tucked away like old memories in the back of the drawer because society says they're not supposed to be the mark of a good or balanced human, yet each one holds a piece of our soul, longing to be acknowledged and embraced. It takes immense courage to peel back the layers and accept them, but it's a journey worth taking.

Well, it's time to dust off those emotions and give them a spotlight! Middle-aged women? They've got a front-row seat on the emotional rollercoaster of hormones, family drama, and work woes. Talk about a balancing act! But is it acknowledging and dealing with these emotions? That's the secret to keeping our sanity intact. So, here's to embracing the thrill of being human. After all, life's too short for emotional repression and too long for pretending we've got it all figured out! It's okay not to have all the answers, to stumble and fall, because that's part of the journey, too.

In this section, I want to voice the suppressed emotions we all feel but never express. It's an intensely personal and silent struggle I've felt within myself and witnessed in others I know. These emotions linger in the shadows of our hearts, yearning to be heard, understood, and accepted. They're not just my feelings of pain and unspoken fears; they're ours, connecting us and reminding us that we are never alone on this journey.

The Green-Eyed Monster:
ENVY

"Envy is the art of counting the other fellow's blessings instead of your own."

— **Harold Coffin**

*F*or me, it all began with school and college reunions—an exciting opportunity to reconnect with old friends and classmates. The joy of meeting them was unparalleled, but afterwards, comparison reared its ugly head. It seemed like everyone had achieved outstanding success in their careers, but despite possessing talent, potential, and education, I felt like I hadn't done anything much in life.

Upon returning home from one of these reunions, my husband innocently asked me about the event, and in a self-deprecating moment, I blurted out, "I've not done anything useful in my life!" Then, to add insult to injury, my son demanded dinner. I completely lost my self-control, exclaiming that all my youthful years had been devoted to nothing more than a janitor's role—cleaning and washing.

The following week was a whirlwind of depression and worthlessness. However, in a sudden burst of determination, I decided that though I might have wasted my life so far, I wouldn't waste any more. Ideas for business models, professional courses, and endless educational pursuits flooded my mind. It became a comical situation as my qualifications multiplied so much that they could no longer fit in a simple biodata.

Yet, despite my newfound expertise, finding a permanent job remained an area for improvement. Perhaps it's because, with the constant moving and changing of houses—two or three times yearly—who would be willing to offer me employment? So, I opted to become a freelancer—an ironic choice where "freelance" meant working for free initially. It's like having a job in your free time, except your services are uncompensated.

Oh, this journey! I started navigating the dangerous path of freelancing, armed with numerous qualifications and a determination to break the cycle of constant change. Who knows what the future holds, but at least I am trying to follow my newfound dream of doing something significant with my life.

Women have this peculiar habit of relentless comparison. They need to be more content with themselves and their lives. Don't get me wrong; I always defend them, arguing that growth becomes stagnant without comparing and aiming for better things. But, oh boy! I've fallen prey to this jealousy bug, especially when witnessing others flourish in their careers.

However, as the sands of time slipped through my fingers, something profound dawned upon me. People look up to me for the remarkable family and relationships I've built. Who would have thought? Here I was, green with envy over career achievements, while all along, my actual value lay in the bonds I've nurtured and the love I've shared.

Yes, it's a twist, indeed. While I obsessively eyed others' professional triumphs, little did I know that I had carved out a niche as the maven of family dynamics and the connoisseur of heartwarming connections. It's like being crowned the queen of relational social wonders while wondering which job title to print on my business cards.

Ah, the profound wisdom that has finally dawned upon me! Having it all in this vast and unpredictable world seems as vague as trying to walk two paths simultaneously. It would help if you, my dear friends, made choices.

But wait, hold up! As I reflect on my past, I've had an eye-opening realisation. That person I used to envy for their seemingly impeccable career? They lived in a joint family, with wise elders shouldering the weight of child-rearing. Imagine the chaos they had to manage behind the scenes! And what about that other girl who appeared to be soaring in her career? Little did I know, she was the sole breadwinner, forced to excel due to familial circumstances.

Oh, the irony! There I was, fixated on the shiny

exterior of their lives, completely ignorant of the intricate tales woven beneath the surface. It's a universal foible, my friends—judging by appearances alone. We often disregard the sweat, toil, and countless hours hidden behind enviable physiques, jaw-dropping successes, and seemingly perfect lives.

So, let this be a lesson for our envious hearts. The next time that green-eyed monster creeps in let's pause and dive deeper into the untold stories. Who knows, that remarkable physique we envy may have required countless gruelling hours at the gym and a diet that banishes all joy from one's taste buds!

Dealing with envy and jealousy can be quite a challenge. You know those moments when you spot a friend's flashy new car, and suddenly, your vehicle feels outdated? Or when scrolling through social media, it seems like everyone is living their best life while you're stuck in your pyjamas, binge-watching Netflix? It's enough to stir up a storm of frustration. But before you let those feelings spiral out of control, take a moment to give yourself credit for recognising them. Admitting that you're envious isn't easy and is a crucial first step.

Envy and jealousy are natural reactions that can emerge when we compare ourselves to others or feel inadequate in some aspect of our lives. Although these emotions are common, they can take a toll on our well-being if we don't address them. Start by acknowledging your feelings rather than hiding them away. Reflect on what triggers your envy—whether it's someone's achievements, possessions, or relationships.

Understanding these triggers can provide insight into your desires and goals.

Instead of seeing envy as an opposing force, reframe it as an opportunity for personal growth. Let it drive you to identify areas where you'd like to improve. Cultivate gratitude by focusing on the positives in your life and appreciating your unique journey. Keeping a gratitude journal can help shift your perspective and highlight the good.

Social media often exacerbates these feelings by showcasing only the highlight reels of others' lives. Consider limiting your time on social media or curating your feed to include accounts that inspire and uplift you rather than ones that fuel comparison. Building self-confidence and celebrating your achievements can also help counteract envy. Pursue hobbies, learn new skills, and engage in self-care to boost your self-esteem.

Empathy can be a powerful antidote to envy. Recognise that everyone faces their struggles and celebrate their successes with a genuine heart. Shifting your focus from comparison to compassion can reduce resentment and foster positive connections. Seek inspiration from those you admire, using their achievements as motivation to pursue your own goals.

Finally, if envy becomes overwhelming or persistent, don't hesitate to seek support from friends, family, or a therapist. They can offer valuable perspectives and help you navigate your emotions. Remember, each person's journey is unique, and comparing yourself to others only hinders your progress and happiness.

Embrace your individuality, focus on your growth, and celebrate the successes of others without letting envy or jealousy consume you. In this journey of comparisons, remember there's more to a person's story than meets the eye. So, my dear friends, grab that book of life, flip through its pages, and discover the untold stories that shape our desires. And who knows, we'll find solace in our own unique stories.

Key Points

Three Ways to Fight the Green-Eyed Monster

Gratitude Journaling:

Pick a time and sit with your journal every day. Just before bed is ideal to close out the day on a positive note. Write down three things that happened in the day that made you happy or feel grateful. Nothing is too small to highlight; the most straight forward things also count.

Social Media:

Limit your time with doom scrolling. To control how much content you consume, you can begin by setting a timer and adhering to it.

Phone a Friend:

If you find yourself spiralling, call a friend and ask them to help redirect your focus to all the things that are working in your life.

I Am Not Alone, but
LONELY

"Loneliness is not a lack of people, but a lack of connection."

– Anonymous

Natasha, her husband, and their two teenage children formed a modern-day family unit. Their lives seemed to follow a predictable routine, yet underneath the impression of togetherness, a profound sense of loneliness plagued each family member uniquely. Despite craving meaningful connections outside her family, Natasha sought solace and friendship from her husband and children. However, their constant distractions and busyness left her feeling unheard and isolated. Her husband, burdened by work and personal concerns, found temporary escape in the flickering lights of the television and the alluring realm of social media. Instead of addressing the disconnect in their marriage, he chose virtual validation over engaging in heartfelt conversations, further deepening his sense of loneliness.

Yearning for understanding and acceptance, the teenage children turned to their virtual friends and online platforms for companionship. These digital interactions offered a reprieve but ultimately left them detached and more alone. Their pleas for attention and empathy often went unnoticed in the virtual realm. In an attempt to fill the void within, Natasha found herself increasingly drawn to social media. She sought comfort in the fabricated connections it offered, unaware that it only added to her sense of emptiness and loneliness. Each member of the family was physically present but mentally and emotionally distant, and as time passed, the family's emotional chasm widened, deepening the feeling of isolation.

Loneliness is more than being alone; it is a deep emotional state that can leave us feeling isolated, disconnected, and empty. It's not just about physical distance or solitude; it's a longing for meaningful social and emotional connections that bring joy and fulfilment.

When loneliness creeps in, it can make us feel like we're standing on the outskirts of life, watching others form bonds and share laughter while we feel invisible. It can leave us yearning for someone who truly understands and accepts us and makes us feel seen and valued.

Various circumstances can trigger it—the absence of close relationships, a breakdown in existing connections, or feeling disconnected from the world around us. It can happen when people surround us, yet we still feel emotionally detached. Loneliness can make us question our worthiness of love and belonging, intensifying our sadness and isolation.

But it's important to remember that loneliness is a universal experience, something we all encounter at different times, like middle-aged women.

As women navigate the path of marriage, it often entails leaving behind childhood friendships, moving to their partner's address, and immersing themselves in the whirlwind of family life. Time becomes a precious commodity. And it becomes challenging to maintain and nurture meaningful connections beyond their spouse's social circle. As the years go by, children grow up and leave the nest, and the dynamics within their relationships may change. If a woman has invested in her partnership, she can use open communication and shared experiences to weather the storms that inevitably arise. However, if that foundation isn't strong, the relationship can become mundane, tinged with feelings of disconnection.

Suddenly, a woman finds herself with an empty nest, few meaningful friendships, and a growing sense of isolation. She may feel invisible even in a crowded room as if her voice is unheard and her needs are misunderstood. Loneliness becomes a constant companion.

Being alone is different from being lonely. Being alone refers to a physical state of being by oneself, often in the absence of other people. It could be by choice or circumstance and doesn't necessarily indicate a negative or distressing experience. Some individuals enjoy and seek out moments of solitude, finding it rejuvenating and essential for self-reflection, creativity, and personal growth.

On the other hand, loneliness is an emotional state that arises from a perceived lack of connection, meaningful relationships, or intimacy. It goes beyond physical solitude, encompassing isolation, sadness, or a deep longing for companionship.

Understanding the distinction between the two is crucial. Being alone can be a positive and empowering choice, giving individuals the opportunity for self-discovery and personal growth. Loneliness, on the other hand, can have negative consequences on mental health and overall well-being if it persists and becomes chronic.

In today's modern world, the decline of real-world interactions and the rise of distant communications and social media have left many dissatisfied and longing for genuine human contact. Even in families where multiple members exist under the same roof, there needs to be more meaningful interaction, as everyone tends to spend their free time absorbed in social media or in front of screens, leading to individuals feeling lonely in their separate rooms.

Many middle-aged women grapple with feelings of loneliness. However, there are ways to navigate this phase of life and create meaningful connections that can alleviate the sense of isolation.

One crucial step is actively working on relationships, especially within the family. Spending precious minutes daily to provide a listening ear without judgment and undivided attention can work wonders. It's important to recognise our role in this shift, as we often turn to electronic devices to entertain our children instead of genuinely engaging with them by listening to their stories, complaints, and triumphs. Through these genuine interactions, actual bonds are formed, and neglecting to prioritise them can lead to a generation where virtual feelings and interactions overshadow the nourishing, authentic connections our souls genuinely crave.

Instead of devoting those few moments of free time to social media, redirect the focus towards each other. Invest in creating memories with extended family members, as they often share common values and can provide an understanding support network. Exploring hobbies can also be an excellent avenue to find like-minded individuals and develop new friendships. Rather than seeking validation solely from your husband's friends, acquaintances, or coworkers, embrace opportunities to participate in activities that bring you joy and allow genuine connections to flourish.

Travelling to unfamiliar places, such as embarking on a hiking adventure, can be transformative. When removed from the distractions of daily life and faced with the need to converse with one another, these experiences can foster a sense of shared accomplishment and facilitate deeper emotional connections. In these moments of vulnerability and shared experiences, bonds are forged, contributing to an improved sense of belonging and fulfilment.

Acknowledging and addressing feelings of loneliness is essential in the journey through middle age. By actively working on relationships, embracing genuine connections, and fostering meaningful experiences, women can navigate this chapter of life with greater emotional well-being and find solace in genuine connections that nourish their souls.

Natasha was battling loneliness without even being aware of it. She had become so comfortable being stuck in a safe, lonely place that she did not want to come out, confusing it with solitude. Therefore, for women like Natasha, change can only come when they recognise the pattern and take proactive steps by working towards meaningful connections and relationships.

Key Points
Five Ways to Battle Loneliness
1. Acknowledge your emotions
2. Work on your close relationships and make memories together
3. Develop new hobbies and friendships
4. Travel and experience the world
5. Limit your social media time

Whispering of the Soul
DEPRESSION AND MOOD SWINGS

Once upon a time, in the land of domestic bliss, a lady could be seen gently sipping her tea, peering out of her window, and basking in the glow of her blessed life. With a doting husband, healthy children, understanding in-laws, and her beloved parents still by her side, she couldn't help but thank the heavens for the abundance of love surrounding her. Her home was always bustling, brimming with the laughter and company of loved ones.

However, as the fickle tides of fate would have it, this very same lady underwent a curious transformation in just a few days. Suddenly, she found herself irritated beyond measure. Her once-praiseworthy husband was now labelled "hopeless" and "never helpful." Her children, once the apple of her eye, had become masters of taking her for granted. To make matters worse, her in-laws had intensified their meddling ways, and even her parents seemed to favour her less-than-perfect spouse. The lady had reached her wit's end, and her frustration became the soundtrack of her home. It appeared the tiniest of inconveniences would trigger a storm of shouting and scolding.

Now, one may wonder, what in the realm of chaos could have caused such a twist in her demeanour? Is a wicked force manipulating her emotions with dark magic at play? Well, dear reader, fear not, for the answers lie within biology. For you see, our hormonal companions wield significant control over our emotions. In this case, the mighty progesterone is to blame.

Progesterone, a calming and sedating hormone, stabilises our moods and sleep. But alas, during those tumultuous times of perimenopause and PMS, it tends to bid us farewell, leaving us in a state of hormonal disarray. Suddenly, the once-tranquil lady finds herself caught in a storm of irritability.

Thus, dear reader, we learn that even the most blessed lives can be subject to the whims of hormones. Let us approach this tale with empathy, for life's twists and turns have a way of shaking even the sturdiest people. This is something common that most ladies experience during this transition.

On a serious note, understanding depression during menopause and perimenopause is crucial. It can be a complex condition that often gets misconstrued as ordinary menopausal symptoms. Distinguishing between clinical depression and the natural mood swings associated with menopause can be challenging.

Do you find yourself experiencing sudden feelings of sadness, particularly in your early to mid-40s, alongside changes in your menstrual cycle? This may be more closely related to menopause. Mood fluctuations are expected during the various stages of menopause, including perimenopause, menopause itself, and post-menopause.

Clinical depression, on the other hand, involves intense and prolonged feelings of despair that significantly impact your daily life. It can leave you feeling overwhelmed, hopeless, and devoid of self-worth, making it difficult to function normally.

Depression can manifest at any stage of the menopause transition, which is why it's vital to pay attention to any noticeable changes in yourself or others around you. Familiarising yourself with the symptoms can help you identify depression:

- Disturbed sleep patterns

- Changes in appetite

- Constant fatigue

- Restlessness or agitation

- Difficulty concentrating or making decisions

- Feelings of worthlessness or excessive guilt

- Persistent thoughts about death or mortality

Suppose you ever find yourself experiencing thoughts of self-harm or suicide, seeking immediate assistance from a mental health specialist or helpline is imperative.

Remember, depression is not something you have to face alone. Contact your family, friends, or professionals who can provide emotional support and professional guidance to help you navigate this challenging period.

Depression during perimenopause and menopause is influenced by a combination of factors, making it difficult to pinpoint a single cause for low mood and depressive symptoms. Hormonal factors play a significant role in this process, and it is important to remember that these changes do not reflect personal weakness. Several studies have linked hormone fluctuations to changes in mood and anxiety. For example, estrogen, one of the primary hormones affected during menopause, is tied to serotonin levels, often called the "happy hormone." When estrogen levels decrease, serotonin levels may also decrease, potentially contributing to low mood.

Additionally, estrogen has been found to influence cortisol levels, which is known as the hormone of stress. When estrogen levels decline, cortisol levels may rise. The sensitivity of individual brains to these hormonal changes varies.

Have you previously experienced postnatal depression or more severe forms of depression? In that case, you may be more susceptible to mood changes during menopause. It is crucial to be aware of this, as declining estrogen levels can reduce your resilience to stress and potentially exacerbate depressive symptoms.

Understanding these connections can help you remain vigilant for changes in your mood and seek help earlier rather than later. It's essential to reach out for support when needed and not hesitate to seek assistance from healthcare professionals.

Treating depression is a challenging journey, but there is hope for healing and finding happiness again. It's crucial to remember that you are not alone in this battle, and reaching out for help takes immense strength and courage.

When depression casts its dark shadow over your life, making simple lifestyle changes can make a significant difference. Regular exercise, even if it's just a short walk, can boost your sense of well-being and provide a glimmer of happiness amidst the darkness. You may find that movement and physical activity improve your body and nourish your soul.

Finding peace within yourself can feel like an impossible task in the depths of despair. However, mindfulness, yoga, and meditation can gently guide you towards soothing your troubled mind and finding solace. These practices allow you to reconnect with the present moment, offering a respite from the overwhelming thoughts and emotions that engulf you.

While it may be tempting to turn to alcohol as a temporary escape, it ultimately exacerbates your low mood. It disrupts your sleep, leaving you even weary and sad the next day. It's essential to be mindful of the impact alcohol can have on your mental well-being and seek healthier coping mechanisms.

The power of talking should always be considered. Sharing your struggles with a professional, such as a therapist trained in cognitive-behavioural therapy (CBT), can provide invaluable insight and support. Through counselling or coaching, you can explore the roots of your depression, challenge negative thought patterns, and develop empowering strategies to break free from the cycle of despair.

Sometimes, despite all efforts, depression persists and refuses to loosen its grip. In such cases, medication, like antidepressants, may be necessary. These medications work to restore balance to the brain's chemistry, providing a lifeline for those enduring persistent, long-term, or severe depression. It's crucial to consult with a compassionate healthcare professional who can guide you in finding the most suitable treatment option for your unique circumstances.

Throughout this challenging journey, support is vital. Self-compassion and seeking solace in embracing loved ones can provide a sanctuary of healing. Prioritise your well-being, nourishing your body, mind, and soul gently.

Disclaimer: The above information provided is solely for informational purposes. It does not substitute professional medical advice, diagnosis, or treatment. If you believe you may be experiencing depression or any mental health condition, seeking assistance from a qualified therapist or psychiatrist who can create an individualised treatment plan for your specific needs is crucial. This disclaimer emphasises the importance of consulting with a healthcare professional for accurate diagnosis and guidance rather than relying solely on the information provided here or elsewhere.

Key Points
If you suspect you might be depressed:
1. Identify your symptoms.
2. Talk to trusted family or friends who can offer empathy.
3. Include exercise, yoga and meditation in your daily routine.
4. Avoid alcohol.
5. If depressive symptoms persist, seek guidance from a mental health expert.
6. If you have suicidal thoughts, contact emergency services immediately.

Banishing
BOREDOM

"Boredom is the experience of one's self in an unproductive state."

– Erich Fromm

I am the perpetual boredom connoisseur, constantly seeking change, engaging in conversations, and having a mind as sharp as a needle to interact with. There are times when I can't help but feel a twinge of envy towards those who effortlessly laze around, seemingly doing nothing. But deep down, I have a sneaking suspicion that behind their idle appearance, they are filled with hidden activity, relishing those rare moments of solitude.

In middle age, as your children and spouse have become self-sufficient, you yearn for more than just the monotonous routine. Everything remains unchanged—your job, the people around you, even your relationships. It's as if time has taken a hiatus, leaving you trapped in a loop of predictability.

However, within this restlessness, something whispers in your ear, calling for growth. You crave something more, whether it's within your relationships or your career. Deep within you lies untapped potential, waiting to burst forth like a radiant flame.

The mischievous little voice of boredom! It's like that friend constantly whispering in your ear, urging you to break free from the chains of routine and embark on wild adventures. And here I am, writing a book! Can you believe it? In my wildest dreams, I never imagined myself as an author, but boredom has its ways of surprising us.

I was stuck at home with my son at a crossroads in his career. Oh, the familiar feeling of restlessness! But instead of succumbing to mind-numbing Netflix marathons, I gave boredom a run for its money. "Fine," I said, "I'll attempt something I've never done before!" And here I am, typing away with the determination of a squirrel on a caffeine high.

It's funny. Boredom, that troublemaker, knows our hidden talents better than we do. It pokes us, prods us, and pushes us to embrace our fears and do the things we're secretly capable of but too afraid to try.

Boredom, ever the catalyst for change, holds the key to uncharted territory. It possesses a profound understanding of our hidden capabilities. By heeding its call and breaking free from our self-imposed limitations, we unveil a world of possibilities we never knew existed.

So, my fellow seekers of excitement, consider the power of boredom. Quiet that voice of fear and embrace the potential within you. Seize the chance to explore new frontiers. Even the most straightforward steps out of our comfort zones can lead to remarkable discoveries. Shed the shackles of routine and let curiosity guide your way. Let boredom awaken the dormant adventurer within you, and together, let us embark on a journey of self-discovery.

Key Points
How to overcome boredom?
1. Recognise that boredom can reveal hidden talents and potential.
2. Challenge the monotony of your daily life by making intentional changes.
3. Use boredom as a catalyst for growth by exploring new activities or pursuing projects.

Repressed
ANGER

"Anger is an acid that can do more harm to the vessel in which it is stored than to anything on which it is poured."

– Mark Twain

Sonali, a 49-year-old financial analyst, was trapped in an unfulfilling marriage, staying with her husband only for the sake of their kids. Each day was a constant, silent battle between them. Over the years, they had grown apart, and the love they once shared had faded, replaced by glaring differences. Yet, they still appeared happily married to the outside world.

Sonali carried herself with grace and warmth, her cheerful smile masking the storm brewing inside her. Her enchanting presence drew people towards her, but in reality, beneath the surface, she was a walking contradiction. Her vibrant exterior symbolised joy and contentment, while her inner world was filled with turbulent emotions she had hidden for years.

These bottled-up feelings manifested in both her body and mind. Tension gnawed at her muscles, migraines plagued her with throbbing pain, and her stomach was always in knots, reflecting the intensity of her unresolved emotions. Emotionally, Sonali lived on the edge, teetering between the tender remnants of who she used to be and the smouldering anger that threatened to consume her. Her rage would erupt like a dormant volcano, leading to unexpected outbursts that made her regretful. Yet, even in these moments, she couldn't fully acknowledge the fury within her, buried beneath layers of self-doubt and fear. She felt trapped by her inability to express her anger, validate its existence, and confront its source, deepening her emotional turmoil. Despite the radiant smile she wore for the world, inside, Sonali was struggling with a profound, silent rage she couldn't escape.

As we age and enter the middle stage of our lives, we may believe that anger becomes a thing of the past. However, an unexpected realisation emerged while listening to a thought-provoking podcast on anger management: the truth is, like Sonali, we haven't stopped feeling anger, but rather, we have become experts at burying and disregarding it. It's almost as if we've constructed a metaphorical cage to imprison our emotions, ensuring they remain unseen by others. The result? We continue our journey, prioritising pleasing others and maintaining societal harmony above acknowledging it.

Anger is a complex emotion that can arise from many causes. For Sonali, it stemmed from emotional abuse and an unfulfilled marriage. However, there are many other triggers. Frustration is one common cause, like when deserving college students face repeated career failures due to family commitments. This frustration builds up and can lead to anger. Perceived injustice, such as unfair treatment or discrimination, can trigger anger. Violating personal boundaries and values, like disrespect or invasion of privacy, can elicit strong emotional responses. Betrayal and hurt, such as infidelity, often result in anger as well. Loss and grief can trigger anger as part of the grieving process, arising from sadness, powerlessness, or a sense of injustice. Feeling threatened or endangered, whether facing physical violence, bullying, or verbal abuse, can evoke anger as a protective response. Accumulated stress from prolonged exposure to stressors like work pressures, relationship difficulties, or financial strains can build up and lower tolerance levels, making individuals more prone to anger outbursts.

In middle life, women often encounter various types of anger that require careful attention. This stage requires addressing unresolved emotional issues, such as past traumas or lingering emotional wounds. Significant transitions like menopause, changes in career or relationships, and the empty nest syndrome can provoke feelings of loss, frustration, and uncertainty. Gender-related anger may arise in response to societal inequalities, sexism, or unfair treatment. Relationship conflicts and long-standing issues can amplify anger during this period.

Recognising and understanding the diverse causes of anger is crucial for developing effective strategies to manage and communicate this powerful emotion. By seeking healthy outlets like constructive communication, therapy, physical exercise, or relaxation techniques, individuals can better navigate their anger and prevent it from negatively impacting their well-being and relationships.

Sonali started by acknowledging her anger and recognising the leading cause of it—her unfulfilled marriage. She and her husband began working together to solve the differences they had developed over the years and bridge the distance between them. She identified her repressed trauma and suppressed emotions through self-reflection, introspection, and seeking external support. She noticed recurring patterns of behaviour, intense emotional reactions, and unexplained triggers that led her to suspect deeper unresolved issues. She paid closer attention to her emotional responses, noticing fluctuations in her mood, unexplained anxiety, and persistent feelings of being overwhelmed or disconnected.

Through self-exploration and reading about trauma and emotional repression, Sonali started to connect the dots between her past experiences and her current emotional struggles. With the support of a therapist, she engaged in deeper conversations, explored her past traumas, and unravelled the layers of her suppressed emotions. Recognising these signs provided valuable insights, and with professional guidance, Sonali found a safe environment to explore and address her underlying trauma. This journey helped her heal and express her anger in healthier ways while also working to improve her marriage.

As Sonali navigated her path to healing, she discovered the strength to confront her buried emotions and rebuild her life. In doing so, she mended her marriage and reclaimed her sense of self. Her journey reminds us that it is never too late to address our pain, embrace our anger, and strive for the happiness we deserve. Middle age is not the end but a new beginning—an opportunity to redefine our lives and find peace within ourselves.

Key Points
How do we deal with repressed anger?
1. Recognise and accept that you are experiencing repressed anger.
2. Open up to trusted individuals or partners about your feelings.
3. Engage in self-reflection and introspection to understand your emotional patterns and triggers.
4. Consult a therapist or counsellor to explore underlying issues and traumas.
5. Use the insights gained from professional support and self-reflection to heal and rebuild yourself.

Letting Go of
GUILT

Seema took a courageous leap by reclaiming her happiness as she no longer wanted to rely on her husband and children for validation and fulfilment. With an excited twinkle in her eye and a newfound sense of liberation, she meticulously planned a day to spend with her friend and to indulge in some much needed "me time." Little did she know that a storm of resistance awaited her upon her return home.

To her utter surprise and horror, instead of being greeted with joy, Seema encountered her husband in full complaining mode and her children unleashing a chorus of howls about the absence of nourishment and parental chauffeurs. Like an unexpected slap in the face, a monstrous wave of guilt crashed over her. Instantly, she embarked on a mission to appease everyone for the "crime" she committed—taking precious time to care for herself.

Ah, the absurdity of societal expectations that dictate women must devote themselves entirely to others, neglecting their own needs. And heaven forbid they dare to seize a few moments to recharge and show themselves some compassion! It's as if self-care is an alien concept, met with bewildered glances and gasps of "How dare she?!" Guilt swarmed around her like a cloud of persistent mosquitoes on a summer's night.

With all her enthusiasm, Seema morphed momentarily into a caped crusader, determined to claim her slice of happiness, only to stumble into the clutches of guilt like a clumsy superhero tripping over her cape. Ah, the never-ending guilt trip of ambitious career women! We strive to soar in our professional pursuits, only to be haunted by guilt about leaving our dear families in the dust. It's like an unwelcome guest that overstays its welcome, lingering in the corners of our minds as we juggle the cosmic balancing act of being supermom-CEO-chef.

To escape that guilt, we become master multitaskers, effortlessly toggling between cooking gourmet meals, tidying up our homes to Pinterest-worthy standards, and showering our loved ones with extravagant gifts. Even when we're running on fumes and can barely keep our eyes open—well, this resembles sleep-deprived zombies more than career powerhouses.

But wait, it doesn't end there! Our adorable offspring, who have grown up witnessing our tireless dedication, have become experts at guilt-tripping, too. Those little terrors have perfected the art of tugging at our heartstrings, mercilessly reminding us that we couldn't witness every crayon scrawl and playground triumph during their formative years. And when we think they've moved on, they strategically resurrect those guilt-inducing memories to get themselves some premium gifts. Overcoming guilt can be an emotional and deeply personal journey for many women. It requires a willingness to confront the inner demons that tell us we are not doing enough or are somehow failing those we love.

To break free from the chains of guilt, we must first acknowledge the weight it carries within our hearts. The guilt we feel as women can be relentless, whispering in our ears during moments of quiet reflection, reminding us of the times we weren't there or couldn't give our all. It can fill our minds with doubts and drown us in a sea of self-blame.

But it's time to release ourselves from this emotional burden. It's time to recognise that we are only human with our dreams, passions, and aspirations. We must learn to extend the same compassion and forgiveness to ourselves that we readily give to others. Overcoming guilt is essential to finding personal happiness and fulfilment as a woman.

Navigating the path of guilt as a woman is not for the faint-hearted. It's like traversing a path fraught with thorns, each prick a reminder of societal expectations and self-imposed standards. Yet, amidst the shadows of doubt, there lies a glimmer of hope—a guide of self-compassion and empowerment waiting to be embraced. Remember, you are strong, resilient, and capable of overcoming these challenges with unwavering determination.

Start by acknowledging the weight of guilt, understanding that it's a shared burden among many women. Challenge its roots in unrealistic standards and societal pressures, daring to question its validity in your life narrative. You deserve to prioritise your well-being to untangle yourself from the chains of guilt that bind you.

Practice self-compassion as if you were tending to a fragile bloom, nurturing it with kindness and understanding. Recognise that you are doing your best and that placing your needs, dreams, and ambitions on a pedestal is okay. It's crucial to allow yourself the luxury of self-care, setting boundaries, and retreating into moments of rest and rejuvenation without guilt anchoring you down.

Reframe your perspective from self-blame to self-empowerment, igniting the flames of ambition and purpose within. See your aspirations and pursuits not as betrayals but as guides leading you towards your most authentic self. Understand the positive ripple effect of your endeavours on yourself and those around you, becoming a source of inspiration and empowerment.

Open the floodgates of communication with your loved ones, allowing vulnerability to bridge the gap between guilt and understanding. Help them see that pursuing your dreams doesn't diminish your love for them. Cultivate a garden of empathy and mutual support within your relationships, where honesty and understanding bloom freely. Your voice matters, and being heard, encouraged, and supported is essential.

Find solace in the arms of a robust support system, drawing strength from the collective embrace of friends, family, and mentors. Share your fears and uncertainties with them, allowing their guidance and encouragement to light the way through the darkness of guilt.

Embrace the imperfection of your journey, understanding that balance and flexibility are the threads weaving the fabric of a fulfilling life. Set realistic expectations, learn to delegate and ask for help when needed, and revel in the joy of small victories. Celebrate your accomplishments with abandon, honouring the resilience that brought you to this moment, and let the echoes of guilt fade into the past.

Remember, overcoming guilt is a journey that takes time and effort. Be patient with yourself, practice self-compassion, and keep focusing on your personal growth and well-being. You deserve to live a guilt-free and joyful life.

Key Points
How to overcome guilt?
1. Recognise the presence of guilt and understand its origins.
2. Embrace the idea that prioritising your well-being, dreams, and aspirations is normal.
3. Foster open and honest communication with loved ones. Share your dreams and goals with them.

4. Help your loved ones understand that pursuing your aspirations does not diminish your love or commitment to them.
5. Seek support from friends, family, and mentors.

REGRET

A few years ago, I was drowning in regret. I regretted marrying someone whose career left little room to pursue my dreams. I wished I had made different choices, like having more children or studying harder to become an IAS officer. These regrets consumed me, making me feel like I had missed life's best opportunities.

Everything changed dramatically when my husband experienced a severe drug reaction and ended up in the ICU. As I watched him fight, I was struck by the fragility of our existence. His recovery felt like a miracle, and in that intense moment, all my previous regrets seemed trivial. My regret transformed into deep gratitude for having him in my life and for his recovery.

When life presents us with choices, each decision becomes a doorway to a new possibility. As we move forward, it's natural to look back and wonder about the paths we didn't take. This sense of regret often arises from imagining how different our lives might be if we had chosen differently.

Regret is an emotional response to a past action or decision you wish had been different. It often involves disappointment, sorrow, or remorse about missed choices or opportunities. Regret can be related to both actions you took and those you didn't take, and it typically arises when you believe that a different choice would have led to a better outcome. It's a standard part of the human experience, reflecting our desire to make the best possible decisions and our struggle with the reality of our past choices.

Regret often settles deep within us, casting a shadow over our emotions and self-worth. It brings a constant loop of "what ifs," where we replay past decisions, and opportunities we wish had seized differently. This internal struggle can lead to persistent sadness, self-doubt, and anxiety, making it hard to trust ourselves or feel good about our choices. In relationships, regret can create distance and tension, as we might withdraw or express our frustrations in ways that hurt those we care about. This emotional strain can cloud our interactions, leading to misunderstandings or conflicts.

Moving past regret can be an intensely emotional journey. Like any other negative emotion, it's crucial to understand the significance of acknowledging that feeling. Facing your regret head-on allows you to honour and validate your experience rather than suppressing it. Acknowledge the weight of your regret and accept that it's a natural part of being human—something everyone experiences.

Forgiving yourself is crucial. Embrace that mistakes are part of life's learning process and that you did what you thought was right at the time. Allow yourself to move past guilt and self-criticism, nurturing a sense of compassion towards yourself.

If your regret involves others, consider reaching out to them. Honest conversations can offer closure and help mend wounds, paving the way for renewed understanding and connection. As you do this, focus your energy on the present moment and the future. Channel your feelings into setting new, positive goals that reflect your values and aspirations, allowing you to transform regret into motivation.

Cultivating gratitude can also shift your perspective. By actively appreciating the positive aspects of your life, you can begin to see beyond past regrets and embrace the beauty and potential in your current and future experiences. Through these steps, you can gently release the hold of regret, allowing yourself to heal and grow in a more hopeful and fulfilling direction.

Next time you find yourself longing for a different path, thinking that your grass could have been greener with other choices, remember this: if you don't nourish and tend to your present life, all you'll be left with are the weeds of regret. The past cannot be changed, but the future is yours. Pour your love, attention, and effort into the here and now. You transform potential regret into a flourishing, vibrant life by nurturing your current opportunities and relationships. Embrace each moment with care, for cultivating the present makes you find peace and fulfilment.

Key Points:
How do you deal with regret?
1. Face your regret head-on and accept it as a natural part of being human.
2. Forgive yourself for past errors, let go of guilt and self-criticism.
3. If your regret involves others, have honest conversations with them.
4. Redirect your energy towards the present moment and future goals.
5. Practicing gratitude helps you see beyond past regrets and embrace the beauty and potential in your present and future experiences.

ATTACHMENT or DETACHMENT

A middle-aged woman named Manisha finds herself grappling with detachment in her marriage and her relationship with her children, which weighs heavily on her heart. Over the years, the once-strong attachment she felt towards her partner and her children seems to have waned, leaving her feeling isolated and disconnected.

The deep connection she once shared with her partner in her marriage has slowly eroded with time. She thought it could be due to the demands of everyday life, the pressures of work, and the complexities of raising a family that have taken their toll. She longs for the intimacy and closeness they once had, but now it feels distant and elusive.

Similarly, her relationship with her children, which was once filled with warmth and love, now feels strained. As they grow older and more independent, their bond has weakened. She misses the days when they would cling to her, seeking comfort and reassurance, and now she struggles to connect with them on a deeper level.

Attachment is the deep emotional bond that connects one person to another, providing a sense of security and support. It plays a crucial role in emotional and social development, influencing how individuals relate to others in various relationships.

On the contrary, detachment distorts oneself emotionally, mentally, or physically from people, situations, or material possessions. In a broader sense, it involves a conscious decision to let go of intense emotional involvement or attachment to maintain balance and inner peace. While detachment might seem like a way to protect ourselves from pain, it often leads to emotional distance and loneliness. When we detach, we create barriers that prevent genuine connection and can make us feel isolated and unfulfilled.

In a spiritual context, detachment refers to releasing emotional, mental, and physical attachments to people, outcomes, and material possessions. This practice fosters inner peace, emotional stability, and freedom from desire and suffering. But is it possible for us to practise detachment in our daily lives?

As worldly beings, we must balance attachment and detachment to lead fulfilling and meaningful lives. Our hearts are naturally designed to bond deeply with those closest to us—our children, spouses, parents, and dearest friends. These relationships are the bedrock of our emotional and psychological well-being and deserve our fullest attachment. Love, care, and presence should be profoundly felt and consistently expressed in these sacred bonds. Simultaneously, we must be more detached from relationships outside our close circle and from material pursuits. This detachment will help us achieve inner peace and contentment, unburdened by external consequences.

However, in today's fast-paced and digitally connected world, we often find ourselves more attached to external distractions—work, social media, material pursuits, and relationships outside our immediate circle. We pour our energy and attention into these areas, sometimes at the expense of our most cherished connections. We chase professional success, seek validation from online interactions, and accumulate material possessions, believing they will bring us happiness. Yet, this often leads to a superficial sense of fulfilment, leaving us emotionally and physically detached from the people who mean the most to us. Women in their midlives can often feel this disconnect.

Entering midlife can stir up a mix of emotions for women, including feelings of detachment, which various factors can trigger. Hormonal changes during menopause can lead to mood swings and fatigue, making women feel disconnected. Physical changes like weight gain and ageing skin can impact self-esteem, adding to this. Life transitions, such as kids leaving home or career shifts, can disrupt routines and prompt women to question their identity and purpose, furthering detachment. Relationship issues and existential questions about life's meaning and legacy can also play a role in this feeling. Alongside these personal struggles, societal expectations can add pressure, complicating the emotional journey of midlife. Nurturing solid bonds and attachments in close relationships during this time requires a deep understanding from partners and loved ones and concerted effort from women themselves. Women can strengthen their connections by actively engaging in open communication, showing appreciation, and spending quality time together. Embracing physical affection, building trust, and supporting each other's growth can also help bridge emotional gaps.

During this transition, women unintentionally withdraw from intimate gestures with loved ones that foster oxytocin release, a hormone crucial for bonding and emotional connection. This lack of intimate gestures can further exacerbate a vicious cycle. Therefore, women in midlife need to recognise this pattern and take proactive steps to nurture their relationships, engage in activities that promote oxytocin release, and seek support to break the cycle of detachment and strengthen emotional bonds with loved ones. Oxytocin, often called the "love hormone," is a potent mediator of social bonding and attachment in both males and females. This intricate neuropeptide promotes trust, empathy, and intimacy and profoundly influences our connection to others. In females, oxytocin's significance extends to reproductive functions and maternal behaviours, highlighting its profound impact on nurturing relationships. Through its ability to foster feelings of security and warmth, oxytocin plays a pivotal role in shaping attachment styles. Individuals with higher levels of oxytocin often experience secure attachments marked by trust, open communication, and emotional support in relationships. Conversely, lower levels of oxytocin may contribute to insecure attachment patterns, leading to difficulties in forming and maintaining healthy connections.

How can you remain deeply connected without feeling hurt? This question often arises when emotional vulnerability and relationship dynamics are tested during challenging times.

1. Draw Boundaries

- **Create Emotional Space**: Establishing boundaries is essential for emotional health. It means identifying and protecting your limits to feel safe and respected. For instance, you might need to limit your time on work-related tasks or define how much personal space you need.

- **Communicate Needs**: Clearly articulate your needs and limits to others. This involves expressing acceptable and unacceptable behaviours so your relationships can be based on mutual respect and understanding. For example, if constant texting during personal time is bothersome, communicate this calmly and clearly.

- **Ensure Respect**: Boundaries help others understand how to treat you, promoting healthier interactions. Establishing clear guidelines fosters a sense of respect and understanding in your relationships, reducing the likelihood of feeling overwhelmed or disrespected.

2. Reduce Expectations

- **Embrace the Present**: Rather than focusing on how things should be or what you hope to achieve, practice appreciating what is. Enjoy the present moment and acknowledge the current state of your relationships. This shift in focus helps you accept and find joy in the reality of your interactions.

- **Shift to Gratitude**: Replace rigid expectations with a mindset of gratitude. You foster a more positive and accepting outlook by appreciating what you have and what others contribute. For instance, instead of expecting frequent grand gestures from loved ones, value the small, everyday acts of kindness and effort.

- **Open to Reality**: Accepting reality as it is, without imposing idealised expectations, allows you to build stronger and more authentic connections. This acceptance can lead to a deeper appreciation of the people in your life and a more harmonious relationship dynamic.

3. Not Lose Yourself

- **Protect Your Identity**: Nurture your individuality and personal values to maintain a strong sense of who you are. It's important not to lose yourself in someone else's world or demands. Ensure that you continue to pursue your interests and maintain your identity.

- **Nurture Passions**: Engage in activities and hobbies that are meaningful to you. Pursuing your passions and maintaining your personal goals help you stay grounded and fulfilled, enhancing your ability to connect with others while remaining true to yourself.

- **Celebrate Uniqueness**: Embrace and celebrate what makes you unique. By staying true to your beliefs and values, you contribute positively to your relationships and enhance your emotional connections. This self-awareness and authenticity make your interactions more genuine and enriching.

Integrating these expanded practices into your life allows you to cultivate deep, meaningful relationships while safeguarding your emotional well-being. This approach will enable you to experience and appreciate the richness of your connections, enhancing both your personal and interpersonal fulfilment.

In a world where non-living entities and many other living beings tread without the burden of feelings, we stand apart, bearing the gift and the weight of our emotions. We find the richness of our humanity through our ability to feel deeply, love fiercely, weep with abandon, and rejoice uncontrollably.

Key Points
1. Balance deep attachment to close relationships with a healthy detachment from external distractions and material pursuits.
2. Women in midlife may experience feelings of detachment due to hormonal changes, life transitions, and societal pressures.
3. To stay deeply connected without emotional distress, establish clear boundaries, reduce rigid expectations, and protect your individuality.

Overcoming
FEAR

As far back as I can remember, I've always been a courageous little girl and a fearless young adult. I was revolutionary, the first to paraglide, to hop on a train without knowing its destination, or to pick fights on the street. I never feared anything—people, sickness, or circumstances. Maybe it was the arrogance of youth, but I believe it was because I always knew my father had my back. No matter what happened, he protected me and pulled me out of trouble.

But everything changed after I got married. Suddenly, I began to develop fears—lots of them. Moving to a new place without friends or family and with my husband often away made me feel isolated and vulnerable. Waking up in the middle of the night in an empty house with no one to turn to if something went wrong filled me with a deep fear of being alone and of the unknown. This once fearless, adventurous spirit now grappled with anxiety and uncertainty, struggling to find the courage that once came so naturally.

When my son was born and diagnosed with a severe illness, my fear deepened. Looking after him alone made me a terrified young mother with no help and a sick child. Even now, thinking about it makes me tremble with fear. I became overly cautious and protective, and even now, when he's 17, I worry endlessly when he comes home late. If that's not all, the COVID pandemic hit, followed by the lockdown. It was a horrifying experience, being left alone with my son in a new town and a new house with no gas, TV, internet, or clean water. My husband was sent on deployment, and fear gripped me completely. I felt it was my duty to protect everyone, and by the time it ended, I nearly had a nervous breakdown. Then, out of sheer frustration, I faced my fears one at a time. It's a long, emotional journey to heal, but I am determined to overcome them and find my strength again.

Fear develops over time through experiences and memories. Have you ever seen a little child fearful of danger? They are naturally fearless and protecting them becomes a mother's duty. But to truly learn, they must face and grow from danger. In these moments of facing the unknown, they begin to understand and develop caution. Watching this transformation can be heartwarming and heartbreaking as the innocence of fearlessness gives way to life's lessons. It reminds us how life shapes us, moulding our bravery into wisdom through each challenge and encounter.

Fear is a powerful and primitive human emotion that arises in response to perceived danger or threat. It triggers a range of physical and psychological reactions, such as increased heart rate, rapid breathing, heightened alertness, and a strong urge to either confront the threat (fight) or escape it (flight). Fear can be a protective mechanism, helping to keep us safe from harm and a learned response based on past experiences and memories. It can be rational, like fear of a dangerous situation, or irrational, like fear of something that poses no real threat. Fear is integral to the human experience, profoundly shaping our behaviour and decisions.

Fear can manifest in various forms, each affecting us differently. Here are some common types:

Biological Fear: This innate response protects us from immediate threats. For instance, the fear of snakes or spiders triggers an automatic reaction to avoid these potentially dangerous creatures.

Conditioned Fear: This fear develops through association with a past negative experience. For example, a person who has a dog bite as a child may grow to fear all dogs as a result of that traumatic incident.

Developmental Fear: Common in children, this fear is a normal part of growth. An example is a young child's fear of the dark, which usually fades as they mature and gain a better understanding of their environment.

Social Fear: This involves anxiety about social interactions and self-image. For instance, someone with social anxiety disorder might feel intense fear about public speaking due to worries about being judged or embarrassed.

Existential Fear: This fear concerns deep, fundamental issues like mortality or life's meaning. A person may experience existential anxiety when contemplating their death or questioning the purpose of their existence.

Phobias: These are intense, irrational fears of specific objects or situations. Acrophobia, or the fear of heights, can cause significant distress when someone is near high places, even if there is no real danger.

Traumatic Fear: This fear stems from past traumatic experiences. For example, a veteran with PTSD might experience severe anxiety and panic when exposed to stimuli that remind them of combat, such as loud noises.

Anticipatory Fear: This involves excessive worry about future events. A person might feel intense anxiety before a major job interview, fearing failure or adverse outcomes even before the event takes place.

Cultural Fear: Influenced by cultural beliefs and practices, this fear reflects societal norms. In some cultures, fear of supernatural beings or adherence to certain taboos can profoundly affect how individuals respond to related situations.

As middle-aged women, several fears often come to the forefront—many worry about their health, facing concerns about ageing and potential illnesses that could impact their well-being. There's also the fear of losing their youthful vitality and struggling with changes in appearance and self-esteem. Financial worries about retirement and job security can cause anxiety about the future. Transitioning to an empty nest can bring a deep sense of loss and questions about one's purpose when children leave home. Relationship changes, whether due to shifts with a partner or changes in friendships, can lead to feelings of isolation. Reflecting on life's meaning and facing the reality of mortality can also be daunting. These fears are deeply personal and emotional, intertwined with the challenges and changes that come with this stage of life.

Overcoming fear as a middle-aged woman can start with acknowledging that fear is a natural part of life. For example, if you feel anxious about your health as you age or experience existential fear about life's meaning, begin by accepting that these fears are common and part of the human experience. Identify what worries you explicitly, such as concerns about developing a chronic illness or questioning your purpose and learn more about these issues to gain a better understanding. Educate yourself about preventive measures and treatment options for health concerns and explore philosophical or spiritual resources to address existential questions.

Challenge any negative thoughts, like fearing that

ageing will inevitably bring serious health problems or that you haven't achieved your life's purpose. Replace these thoughts with more balanced ones, such as understanding that many people age healthily with proper care and that finding purpose can be a continuous journey that evolves.

Take gradual steps to face your fears. For health-related anxieties, start a new exercise routine or schedule regular check-ups. For existential fears, engage in activities that bring you joy or fulfilment and explore new interests or passions that can provide a sense of purpose.

To manage anxiety, practice relaxation techniques like deep breathing exercises or meditation. These practices can help calm your mind and provide clarity. Reach out for support from friends, family, or a therapist who can offer encouragement and practical advice. Engage in discussions about your existential concerns with supportive individuals or join groups that explore similar topics.

Set realistic goals for yourself, such as adopting healthier lifestyle habits or setting aside time for personal reflection and growth. Celebrate each small achievement, like completing a health workshop, sticking to a fitness plan, or gaining new insights into your purpose. Develop a plan to manage situations that trigger your fears, like preparing questions for a doctor's appointment or setting time aside for personal reflection.

Lastly, remember that overcoming fear is a journey, and treating yourself with kindness and patience can make the process more manageable and empowering.

Key Points
How to overcome your fear?
1. Acknowledge and accept your fear.
2. Identify specific fears and gather information about them.
3. Address and replace negative thoughts with more balanced perspectives.
4. Take gradual action.
5. Reach out to friends, family, or a therapist for support and practical advice.

Acknowledging
GRIEF

> *"Grief is the last act of love we have to give to those we love. Where there is deep grief, there was great love."*
>
> **- Catherine Ingram**

When Lata's father passed away suddenly, the loss was overwhelming. At 44, she wasn't very young, but she was still her father's cherished daughter, the apple of his eye even after marriage and children. Her father had been her unwavering pillar, the solution to every problem, from finding a job to babysitting her children, from shifting houses to building her own. His presence was her constant, a steadfast anchor in the stormy seas of life. With his unexpected departure, a heavy mantle of responsibility descended upon her shoulders. As the eldest, she had to take charge, caring for her family, supporting her mother, managing her father's finances, and handling every duty he had left behind. She had to project strength, concealing sorrow, even as her heart ached with the loss of the man who had been her rock and guide.

As time passed, Lata managed to handle all her responsibilities with remarkable strength and competence, but something inside her irrevocably changed. The wound of her father's death remained painfully fresh, an unhealed scar on her heart. Though she appeared composed and resilient on the outside, internally, she struggled with an unending ache. She avoided speaking about her father or his passing, as each mention rekindled the raw pain she carried within. But unlike other people, where time heals the loss of dear ones, why was Lata not able to heal herself from her father's death?

When Lata lost her father, she couldn't bring herself to grieve, and the unexpressed sorrow silently corroded her spirit, leading to profound consequences. The shock and denial of his sudden death acted as a shield, preventing the overwhelming pain from surfacing. As the eldest, societal pressures and cultural norms compelled her to mask her grief, believing that showing vulnerability would undermine her role as the family's pillar. She thought she needed to stay vital for her mother, children, and everyone else, pushing her emotions aside. The fear of facing the raw pain of losing her father made her avoid grief altogether. Yet, this suppression led to severe emotional and mental health issues. Lata's sorrow remained fresh, leading to prolonged grief disorder, depression, and anxiety, leaving her feeling perpetually numb and disconnected. The unresolved grief manifested in physical ailments and chronic stress, silently impacting her health. Her relationships suffered as she withdrew and isolated herself, unable to connect deeply with her loved ones. Her cognitive functions and productivity declined, burdened by the unaddressed sorrow. Ultimately, by not grieving, Lata trapped herself in a perpetual cycle of pain, unable to heal or move forward, the shadow of her father's loss ever-present in her life.

Grief is a natural and emotional response to loss. It can arise from various types of losses, such as the death of a loved one, the end of a relationship, the loss of a job, or a significant life change. The grieving process is how individuals cope with and work through their grief. It is a complex and personal experience that can vary significantly from person to person.

The grieving process typically involves a range of emotions, including sadness, anger, guilt, confusion, and even relief. People may also experience physical symptoms such as fatigue, appetite changes, and difficulty sleeping. Grieving unfolds over time and can be influenced by factors such as the nature of the loss, personal coping mechanisms, past experiences with loss, and the level of support available.

Some different models and theories describe the stages of grief, with the most well-known being the Kübler-Ross model, which outlines five stages: denial, anger, bargaining, depression, and acceptance. It's important to note that not everyone will go through these stages linearly or experience all of them. During the process of grief, initially, you might find yourself in a state of denial, unable to fully grasp the reality of what has happened. You may tell yourself that it can't be authentic or that there must be some mistake. This denial can serve as a temporary shield from the overwhelming pain of loss, a way of protecting yourself from the harshness of reality.

As you come to the truth, anger may wash over you. You may feel a deep sense of injustice, resentment, or frustration at the situation's unfairness. These intense emotions are a natural part of the grieving process as you struggle to make sense of your new reality.

In the bargaining stage, you might find yourself trying to make deals with a higher power or seeking ways to change the outcome. You may think, "If only I had done this differently, things would be better." Bargaining is often a way to regain control when you feel utterly powerless.

Depression may then settle in, bringing with it feelings of profound sadness, loneliness, and regret. It's a time of mourning and reflection, where you confront the total weight of your loss and the impact it has had on your life. It's crucial during this stage to allow yourself to grieve and seek support from loved ones or professionals if needed.

Finally, acceptance may start to dawn. This doesn't mean everything is suddenly fine or the pain has disappeared. Instead, it's a gradual realisation that you can't change what has happened, and you start to find ways to move forward with your life. Acceptance doesn't mean forgetting or being unaffected by the loss but learning to live with it and integrate it into your story.

Long after the passing of her father, Lata embarked on a journey of grieving that led her to confront the deep and complex emotions she had held onto for years. With tear-stained cheeks and a heavy heart, she allowed herself to feel the rawness of loss, to experience the waves of sadness and anger that washed over her. Through moments of solitude and shared tears with loved ones, she found solace in the warmth of human connection and the healing power of shared memories. As she navigated the path of grief, Lata discovered that by honouring her father's legacy, embracing her emotions, and granting herself the space to mourn, she was slowly integrating healing into the fabric of her being. She carried her father's love with her as she embraced the bittersweet beauty of moving forward while still holding him close in her heart.

Key Points
1. People need to grieve when they experience significant losses, such as the death of a loved one, the end of a relationship, etc.
2. Societal and cultural pressures might compel individuals to hide their grief, leading to unresolved sorrow and chronic stress.
3. Unaddressed grief can manifest in physical ailments, chronic stress, and deteriorating mental health, including numbness and isolation.

4. The grieving process typically involves stages such as denial, anger, bargaining, depression, and acceptance, though not everyone experiences them linearly or all of them.
5. Facing and processing grief, honouring the loved one's legacy, and embracing emotions are essential for healing and integrating the loss into one's life.

Part Two
Evolving Relationships

INTRODUCTION

As we journey through middle age, the landscape of our relationships transforms subtly and profoundly. The bonds of marriage, forged through years of shared experiences and challenges, may start to feel like a well-worn garment—familiar and comforting, yet lacking the vibrant intensity they once had. What was once a passionate connection might now seem more like a comfortable companionship, as the demands of daily life overshadow the spark of romance and deep emotional connection.

Our children, who once filled our homes with laughter and chaos, have become independent adults. The physical demands of parenting have eased, but their evolving needs and aspirations continue to tug at our heartstrings. We find ourselves treading the delicate balance of offering guidance while giving them the space they need to forge their paths.

At the same time, our roles with our ageing parents have shifted dramatically. The pillars of strength who once provided us with support and guidance now look to us for care and companionship. Their growing fragility serves as a poignant reminder of the passage of time, urging us to cherish every moment and face the reality of our mortality.

Amidst these changing dynamics, we may also experience a sense of drifting away from childhood friendships and family connections. The bonds with siblings and cousins may have weakened over the years, lapsing into obligatory interactions that lack genuine affection. This midlife period often brings a deep desire to reconnect with these loved ones, relive cherished memories, and mend past misunderstandings. Rebuilding these relationships can offer a profound sense of belonging and solace, reminding us of who we genuinely are amidst life's shifting currents.

As we navigate these evolving relationships in this complex phase of life, searching for connection and renewal becomes a powerful journey. Reconnecting with old friends and family, embracing the comfort of familiar bonds, and nurturing the relationships that matter most can provide grounding and joy, helping us find our way through the intricate changes of middle age.

Made in Heaven
MARRIAGES

Meera, a talented interior designer now in her fifties, married Jai when she was just 23. Over the years, her career flourished, transforming spaces with elegance and warmth while their relationship evolved through various stages of life. Like many long-standing marriages, their journey has been marked by shared dreams, challenges, and the inevitable emotional changes. As Meera reflects on her decades with Jai, her story unveils the common threads that bind many enduring unions. It offers insights and wisdom for other middle-aged women on their marital journeys.

At the onset of her marriage with Jai, Meera's glowing eyes speak of fairytale dreams. Her heart overflows with love, and her mind buzzes with expectations. Ah, the honeymoon phase! During this time, Jai's faults seem like charming traits. Meera showcases her best qualities, and they can't bear to spend a minute apart, utterly enchanted with each other.

But as the honeymoon phase fades and they return to their daily lives, the struggle for dominance emerges. They battle who decides household preferences, from the TV remote to dinner venues and even the thermostat setting, as if competing for supremacy in the jungle.

Exhaustion soon sets in. Meera and Jai realise that this constant struggle is draining. When children come into the picture, they find their time and energy consumed by the little ones. They develop a more cooperative relationship, dividing chores and responsibilities, though occasional disagreements still arise.

As their children grow up and leave home, Meera and Jai suddenly face abundant alone time. During this period, their shortcomings become glaringly visible. Meera, grappling with midlife changes, confronts her unhappiness with a new intensity, seeking to address the deep-seated issues that have surfaced.

When the hormonal influence wanes, the arguments become less frequent. Yet a new issue arises: Meera and Jai no longer experience the same love and passion they once did. Their relationship becomes akin to that of good roommates who have grown accustomed to each other's presence.

Like many long-standing marriages, Meera's story unfolds as a transformation journey. From a young bride's sparkling eyes to a middle-aged woman's tempered wisdom, her experience with Jai provides insights and knowledge for others navigating their marital paths.

In this chapter, we will focus on the effect of middle age on marriages and explore how women's physical and emotional changes can impact their relationships.

Body Image Issues:

During mid-life, women face a series of physical changes due to a decline in estrogen and progesterone levels. As menopause approaches, they may notice weight gain, especially around the waist, along with sagging breasts and the emergence of wrinkles. The once-familiar youthful figure begins to shift, and white hair appears. These transformations can deeply affect body image, leading to issues with self-esteem and feelings of desirability, which can impact their marriage and emotional well-being.

Physical Intimacy:

As women navigate menopause and post menopause, they experience a range of physical and emotional changes that can significantly affect their relationships. The decline in testosterone levels in women around menopause can lead to a reduced sex drive, making it harder to maintain the same level of intimacy as before. Additionally, a decrease in estrogen causes changes in the vaginal tissues, which can lead to physical discomfort during intercourse, further complicating the experience of intimacy. These factors, coupled with fluctuating emotions and body image issues, often result in women withdrawing from physical intimacy, creating a distance that can strain their relationships.

Disconnect:

As a woman faces the physical and emotional changes of midlife, she may begin to withdraw, leading to a breakdown in communication between her and her partner. Frustration can build, and she might raise her voice, not out of anger but as a plea to be heard and understood. Once-frequent physical gestures like hugging and holding diminish, leading to a damaging disconnect. These gestures are no longer there as expected, making it harder to feel connected.

As she feels increasingly isolated in her marriage, her partner also experiences this growing distance, leaving both feeling lost and disconnected.

Loss of Purpose:

Middle-aged women's loss of purpose can impact their relationships. As they reach this stage, many women significantly confront a sense of emptiness or a lack of direction if their primary roles—such as parenting or career responsibilities—have diminished or changed. This loss of purpose can lead to frustration and dissatisfaction, which may spill over into their relationships.

Insights into middle-aged women's experiences during this life stage and the impact of these changes on marriage offer valuable information to implement positive changes. However, this is not a substitute for professional marriage counselling or therapy. Instead, the focus is on how women can work on themselves and their relationships during mid-life. By understanding these challenges, women can find ways to address their emotional and physical changes, fostering growth and connection in their relationships.

Self-Awareness:

Self-awareness is critical to effectively facing challenges in their marriage during midlife. Women can start by understanding and acknowledging the changes they are experiencing, both physical and emotional. Recognising these transitions allows them to address their needs more effectively. Educating themselves about midlife changes—such as hormonal shifts, bodily transformations, and emotional fluctuations— aids in managing these issues. By understanding their experiences, women can proactively adapt and communicate their needs, fostering a more supportive and resilient relationship**.**

Communication:

Communication is vital for middle-aged women and their partners. Openly discussing their feelings and the changes they are experiencing fosters a sense of mutual support. Sharing their emotional and physical challenges helps partners understand each other's struggles and promotes mutual empathy. Discussing issues like hormonal changes, shifts in body image, or feelings of disconnection allows both partners to address concerns together and find solutions. This transparent dialogue fosters emotional intimacy, reduces misunderstandings, and strengthens the relationship, helping both partners navigate midlife transitions as a team.

Self-Care:

Self-care is not a luxury but a necessity for middle-aged women and their marriages. Recognising and addressing your struggles is the first step toward healing. If you're feeling depressed, moody, or anxious, engaging in mindful exercises or talking to a therapist can be immensely beneficial. Gaining weight might signal the need to increase physical activity and to pay closer attention to nutrition. A loss of desire for intimacy calls for an open conversation with your partner and a consultation with your doctor, as there are many ways to address the matter. Prioritising self-care is valuing yourself, enhancing your well-being, strengthening the bond with your partner, and fostering a healthier, more fulfilling relationship.

Financial Security:

Financial security is essential for a woman to feel secure in her marriage. It provides personal stability and confidence, reducing stress and conflicts over money. Women can achieve this security by having a stable job, making intelligent investments, building savings, and owning property. When a woman manages her finances effectively, she can contribute equally to household responsibilities and shared goals, fostering a more balanced and harmonious relationship. This financial independence allows her to approach the marriage from a place of strength and choice rather than compulsion. It also enables her to invest in personal growth and shared experiences, further strengthening the marital bond.

Therapy:

Therapy can be one of the most transformative experiences for couples, especially if you sense deeper problems in your marriage that need attention. Often, we struggle to pinpoint the exact issues that exist, but a marriage counsellor can offer clarity and guidance. They provide a safe space to explore and address underlying problems, offering pathways to healing and understanding. This step, though daunting, can reignite the connection and intimacy that might have faded, leading to a stronger, more resilient bond. Prioritising this effort shows a profound commitment to your relationship, opening doors to renewed love and trust.

Rekindling the spark in your marriage

Imagine your marriage as a beautiful, radiant diamond. Over time, the shine may dim, but you have the power to restore its glow. Just as a jeweller polishes a diamond to bring back its lustre, you and your partner can reignite the magic in your marriage by being intentional and taking action.

Create dedicated time for each other: Make date nights a priority, whether an intimate dinner or a movie night at home. Stepping out of your routine can infuse fresh energy into your relationship. Dressing up for each other shows that you still value your time together.

Find hobbies you both enjoy: Take long walks together to connect on a deeper level. In these moments, share your dreams, desires, and worries. Try something new, whether cooking, dancing, hiking, or painting. Sharing activities creates new memories and strengthens your connection.

Give each other space: Encourage your partner to enjoy a night out with friends while you do the same. Personal time allows for growth and rejuvenation. When you come back together, you'll have new stories to share and a renewed appreciation for each other.

Incorporate the element of surprise: Celebrate each other even when there is no occasion with inexpensive, thoughtful gifts. Fulfil each other's dreams and support each other without being asked to. Simple gestures like a smile, a hug, or a kiss can brighten the other's and maintain warmth in your relationship.

Focus on each other: Your life is more than just the kids or daily responsibilities. Your children will eventually grow up and leave the nest, so nurture the love and partnership that brought you together in the first place.

Practice gratitude and appreciation: One crucial way to reignite the magic is to recognise and acknowledge the qualities and actions you value in your partner. Express your gratitude regularly, whether for taking care of household chores, being a good listener, or simply being there for you.

By incorporating moments of connection, surprise, and appreciation into your marriage, you can maintain a fulfilling relationship that serves as an inspiration to both yourselves, and those around you.

GREY DIVORCES

Maria sat alone in her quiet, sunlit kitchen, staring at the framed photograph on the counter. It was a picture of her and David on their wedding day thirty years ago. She felt a deep pang of sadness and a strange sense of relief. Their marriage had seen its share of joyful moments, but the last few years had been marked by growing emotional distance and unspoken resentment. The children were grown and had left home, and now, it was just the two of them drifting further apart with each passing day.

Maria's journey through divorce began a few months after her youngest daughter left for college. Once filled with laughter and activity, the house now echoed with silence. Maria and David, having devoted their lives to their children and careers, found themselves struggling to reconnect. The realisation hit her hard: they were two strangers living under the same roof.

She tried to rekindle the romance, suggesting trips and new hobbies they could enjoy together. But David seemed indifferent, absorbed in his world. Conversations that once flowed effortlessly now felt forced and awkward. They were both lonely, but neither knew how to bridge the gap that had grown between them.

One evening, after another silent dinner, Maria decided to speak up. With a trembling voice, she expressed her feelings to David. She told him how lonely she felt and how much she missed the connection they once had. David listened, his eyes reflecting the same sadness she felt. He admitted that he, too, was unhappy and didn't know how to fix things. They decided, reluctantly, to see a marriage counsellor.

The counselling sessions were revealing. They unearthed years of unspoken hurts and unmet needs. The counsellor helped them see that they had grown in different directions, each evolving into individuals who no longer fit together as they once had. Despite their best efforts, it became clear that staying together was causing more harm than good.

The decision to divorce was a painful acknowledgement of the end of a long chapter in their lives. But it was also the beginning of a new one. Maria felt fear and hope as she ventured through the unfamiliar terrain of single life at fifty-five. She worried about the financial implications, potential loneliness, and her children's reactions. But she also felt a burgeoning sense of freedom, a chance to rediscover herself.

Maria's divorce was finalised just before her 56th birthday. The process was emotionally draining, and the financial adjustments were challenging. She sold the family home and moved into a cosy apartment in a vibrant part of town. The transition was difficult, but Maria found solace in her newfound independence.

She joined a local book club, something she had always wanted to do but never found the time for. She started painting again, a hobby she had abandoned years ago. She made new friends and reconnected with old ones. Her days were filled with activities that brought her joy and fulfilment.

One afternoon, Maria met Rema at a yoga class. Rema, also recently divorced, shared her story of a grey divorce. They bonded over their shared experiences and became fast friends. Rema introduced Maria to a support group for women going through similar transitions. The group provided a safe space to share, laugh, cry, and heal.

Through these connections, Maria began to see her divorce not as an end but as a new beginning. She realised that it was okay to mourn the loss of her marriage while also embracing the opportunities ahead. Her relationship with David, though changed, became more amicable. They found a way to co-exist peacefully, especially during family gatherings. Though initially shocked, their children supported their decision and appreciated the honesty and courage it took to pursue their happiness.

Maria's health improved as well. The stress and anxiety that had plagued her during the final years of her marriage began to fade. She felt lighter, more energetic, and more in tune with her needs and desires. Prioritising her well-being had profound physical and emotional benefits.

Maria and David's story perfectly describes grey divorce, where couples over 50 decide to part ways, a trend becoming more common. Many factors contribute to this, such as living longer and seeking more happiness, feeling lonely after children leave home, and having financial independence. Retirement can either strengthen or strain a relationship, and society now accepts divorce more than before.

Going through a grey divorce is tough, feeling like you have lost a part of yourself, with significant financial and emotional impact. Health insurance and benefits can be affected, disrupting family relationships and leading to loneliness and isolation.

However, there are positives too. Many find a renewed sense of self and freedom, pursue hobbies and interests, and improve their health. Relationships with ex-spouses can improve, especially when co-parenting. New opportunities and adventures await, allowing individuals to redefine their lives. Seeking help from therapists and counsellors is essential, as is legal and financial planning. Building a support network of friends and family can provide much-needed emotional support, and prioritising self-care and well-being is critical.

Grey divorce is a significant life change with challenges and opportunities. Though difficult and emotional, it offers a chance for personal growth, renewed happiness, and the opportunity to live a life that aligns with one's true desires. It wasn't easy for Maria, and there were days when the loneliness was overwhelming. But she learned to navigate those moments, finding strength in her resilience and the support of her new community. Her journey was evidence that seeking happiness and fulfilment is never too late.

Going through a grey divorce—divorce later in life—can be an emotionally and practically daunting journey but taking thoughtful and strategic steps can help manage the transition and build a secure future.

Legal Assistance:

Engage a lawyer specialising in grey divorce to ensure you receive expert guidance on the legal aspects of your situation. Also, update your will, power of attorney, and beneficiary designations to reflect your new circumstances post-divorce.

Finance:

Consult with a financial advisor to understand how the divorce will impact your financial landscape. They can help you analyse your current financial situation, plan for the division of assets, and create strategies for future economic stability. Analyse how the divorce will affect your financial situation. Collect and organise all essential financial documents, including bank statements, tax returns, investment portfolios, property deeds, and loan agreements. These documents are critical for equitable asset division and a comprehensive financial plan.

Create a Budget:

Develop a budget that reflects your post-divorce financial situation. This involves setting up a detailed plan for managing your income and expenses, taking into account any changes in your financial circumstances, such as changes in living arrangements or income levels. Adjust your budget to accommodate new economic realities. This may involve cutting back on spending, increasing income, or reallocating resources to meet your needs and goals.

Address Health and Insurance:

If you were covered under your spouse's health insurance plan, review your options for obtaining coverage. Ensure adequate health insurance to cover your medical needs. This is crucial for maintaining your health and avoiding financial strain from unexpected medical expenses.

SOLO TRAVELLERS

Maya, Deepa and Sophia are single, but the reasons for their singlehood vary. Whether by choice or circumstance, these women embraced their independence as they traversed their destined paths, discovering that being single allows them to write their own stories.

Maya was entangled in a love affair with her craft. Her devotion to architecture was like a whirlwind romance, leaving little room for the complexities of human relationships. Perhaps her heart belonged not to a person but to the soaring structures she brought to life and her independence.

Deepa was a nurse. Her heart bore the scars of love once cherished and lost as she grew apart from her partner in her marriage. Amidst the remnants of her dreams, she found strength in her newfound independence and peace after separation. Although she embraced singlehood as a shield against further heartache somewhere deep inside, she was still open to finding the right partner.

And then there was Sophia, the vibrant traveller whose soul yearned for adventure and exploration. With each stamp on her passport, she found solace and peace, which left her after the demise of her beloved husband and travel partner. Though her heart may have carried the weight of a departed partner, her spirit soared unfettered, finding peace in the vast expanse of the world.

Many people like Maya, Deepa, and Sophia are single and happy, but regardless of gender, society, with its invisible measuring tape, is always ready to gauge our worth based on the status of our relationships. Our parents, uncles, and aunts especially believe that a single person cannot be happy. But I have still observed the spectacle of women, even men, sticking around in crummy relationships to maintain the illusion of the "Perfect Relationship" to fit in the frame of societal expectations.

In recent years, we have also witnessed the midlife phenomenon of divorces and separations, which hit like a wake-up call. Many financially independent women stop tolerating nonsense and declare, "Enough is enough!" She announces her exit with a flourish, bidding farewell to the chaos.

Being a single woman has become familiar and increasingly accepted and celebrated in today's society. This shift reflects broader changes in cultural norms, economic opportunities, and the evolving understanding of personal fulfilment. Unlike previous generations, where societal expectations tied a woman's worth to her marital status, contemporary women are embracing their independence and the myriad opportunities that come with it. This newfound freedom allows women to prioritise their careers, travel the world, and pursue their passions without the constraints that a traditional relationship might impose.

Emotional resilience is a significant factor in this change. Women today are more empowered than ever to define happiness on their terms. The emotional strength from managing life independently fosters a deep sense of self-worth and confidence.

Moreover, accepting living independently is a testament to the broader societal shift towards individualism and personal freedom. There is a growing recognition that a person's value is not determined by their relationship status but by their character, achievements, and contributions to society.

This understanding allows women to thrive without pressure to conform to outdated societal norms.

Importantly, being alone can often be better than being stuck in a bad relationship. Toxic relationships can drain a person's emotional and physical well-being, leading to stress, anxiety, and a diminished sense of self-worth. Women who choose independence over a harmful relationship are prioritising their mental health and overall happiness.

Although being single offers a sense of liberation and freedom, it also brings challenges. To live a happy and fulfilling life, it's essential to prepare in advance with careful planning.

1. Financial Independence:

- **Budgeting**: Create a detailed budget that tracks your income and expenses. Classify your spending to identify areas where you can save or cut back. Use budgeting tools or apps to help you stay organised and monitor your progress. This discipline ensures that you live within your means and can allocate funds for savings and investments.

- **Investing**: Learn about different investment options such as stocks, bonds, mutual funds, and real estate. Speak with a financial advisor to develop an investment strategy tailored to your financial goals and risk tolerance. Regularly review and adjust your investment portfolio to align with your long-term objectives.

- **Emergency Fund**: Establish an emergency fund that covers three to six months of living expenses. This fund acts as a financial safety net in case of unexpected events like job loss, medical emergencies, or urgent repairs. Keep this money in a separate, easily accessible account, such as a savings or money market fund.

2. Career Development:

- **Set Goals**: Define clear, actionable career goals based on your interests, skills, and long-term aspirations. Break these goals into smaller, manageable steps, and create a timeline for achieving them. Regularly review and adjust your goals as needed to stay on track.

- **Networking**: Build and maintain professional relationships through networking events, industry conferences, and social media platforms like LinkedIn. Networking can provide valuable opportunities for career advancement, mentorship, and collaboration. Be proactive in reaching out to potential contacts and staying engaged with your professional network.

3. Create a Support System:

- **Find Support**: Surround yourself with a network of friends, mentors, and professional advisors who offer guidance, encouragement, and practical support. Seek out mentors who can provide career advice and personal development insights. Building a support network ensures that you have a reliable source of guidance and encouragement during challenging times.

- **Community Involvement**: Engage in community organisations or groups that reflect your interests and values. Whether volunteering, joining clubs, or participating in local events, being active in your community can provide a sense of belonging and purpose. It also creates opportunities to connect with like-minded individuals and build meaningful relationships.

4. Build Strong Relationships:

- **Family Connections**: Stay connected with family members, even if physical distance separates you. Regular communication, whether through phone calls, video chats, or visits, helps strengthen family bonds and provides a supportive network during life's ups and downs.

- **Friendships**: Invest time and effort in cultivating and maintaining deep, meaningful friendships. Regularly connect with friends through social activities, conversations, and shared experiences. Strong friendships provide emotional support, joy, and a sense of connection.

5. Personal Growth:

- **Pursue Hobbies**: Identify and engage in activities that bring joy and fulfilment. Pursuing hobbies allows you to explore your interests, develop new skills, and find satisfaction outside of work and daily responsibilities. Make time for activities that enrich your life.

- **Education**: Invest in your personal development through continuous learning. Everything counts—formal education through degrees or certifications, informal learning through online courses, workshops, or self-study. Expanding your knowledge and skills enhances personal growth and opens up new opportunities.

6. Plan for the Future:

- **Long-Term Goals**: Develop a strategic plan for achieving your long-term goals, including retirement savings, significant purchases, and personal aspirations. Outline the steps needed to reach these goals and set milestones to track your progress. Regularly review and adjust your plan as your circumstances and priorities evolve.

So, my solo adventurers, invest in yourselves like your own personal stock market. This investment might not serve you breakfast in bed, but it's certainly not going to ghost you on a Friday night! Remember, the most incredible love story of all is the one you write with yourself.

Key Points
1. Middle-aged women face physical changes like weight gain, wrinkles, and decreased libido due to hormonal shifts, which can affect body image, intimacy, and overall marital satisfaction.
2. Open and honest communication between partners about their feelings and changes is crucial for mutual support, reducing misunderstandings.
3. Financial stability enhances personal confidence and reduces marital stress, allowing women to contribute equally to household responsibilities and approach their marriage with greater strength.
4. To rejuvenate a marriage, couples should prioritise dedicated time, engage in hobbies, give each other space, incorporate surprises, and practice gratitude and appreciation.
5. Grey divorces refer to separations among couples over 50, often due to increased longevity and evolving personal desires. Although they can be difficult, they can be managed with the help of sound financial and legal advisers and good self-care.
6. Embracing singlehood allows women to explore personal passions, achieve financial independence, and cultivate fulfilling lives despite societal pressures.

FRIENDS

"Friends are the family we choose for ourselves."

- Edna Buchanan

Neeta's life story had all the makings of a heartwarming adventure. Her kids, all grown up and soaring in their pursuits, brought her immense pride and joy, affirming her success as a parent.

Following her separation from her husband—a relationship that had long overstayed its welcome—a wave of relief washed over her, like finally removing a rock from her shoe after a long hike. As for her career, Neeta was the epitome of a successful investment banker, dedicating more time to work than a caffeine addict does to their morning brew.

Finding friends at work turned out to be a challenge. Her authoritative role as the office bigwig left her with more reports than connections, and most men seemed to think she came with an invisible "Hands Off" sign due to her relationship status. So, left to mingle mainly with the ladies, she found herself in a loop of failed attempts at forging emotional bonds.

With time, Neeta realised that work no longer had the same soothing effect. She had a long list of acquaintances but desperately sought that one true friend—someone who'd listen to her, celebrate her wins, and grow with her through life's ups and downs.

Just when Neeta had lost all hope, she stumbled upon an advertisement for a Himalayan hiking retreat. In a moment of spontaneity, she dialled the number and booked a spot. With a mix of nerves, excitement, and hope, Neeta leapt at the unknown, ready for a new chapter filled with adventure, friendship, and self-discovery. Who knew? Perhaps in the hidden valleys of the Himalayas, she'd find the peace and tranquillity she longed for—and the friend she'd been searching for all along.

Finally, the long-awaited day arrived for Neeta to board her flight. She crammed her suitcases until no more would fit, knowing that excess baggage fees would be her inevitable fate. As she landed in Delhi, she hastily grabbed a taxi to the rendezvous point from where the retreat organisers were to collect everyone. Throughout the bumpy taxi ride, she couldn't help but ponder why she had embarked on this journey in the first place.

As Neeta settled into her seat on the bus, she found solace in the sea of smiling faces radiating enthusiasm and passion. It seemed like everyone already knew each other. Choosing a quiet corner, Neeta's solitude was soon interrupted by a fellow passenger who sat next to her just as the bus was about to depart. Despite Neeta's attempts to initiate a conversation, she received only monosyllabic responses. Resigned to the fatigue of the day, she eventually fell asleep. Twelve hours later, she awoke to the breathtaking sight of their destination, ready to embark on a journey that promised to change her life.

Exhausted, Neeta trudged towards her room, only to discover that the same passenger who had sat next to her on the bus was her roommate. Groggily waking up the next day, Neeta initiated a conversation with her roommate, Diana, asking about her origins. Diana hailed from Goa. She was happily married with a six-year-old son and a doting husband. To her surprise, Diana had already brewed a cup of tea for her. They sat together on the balcony on that crisp November day, sipping tea and sharing stories. They forged a bond transcending time and distance, in that serene moment, beginning a deep and lasting friendship.

Over the years, Neeta and Diana's friendship blossomed, evolving into a deep connection that brought them immense joy and solace. They became like sisters from different mothers, and their bond grew stronger daily. Neeta found in Diana a trustworthy confidante, someone she could trust with her innermost thoughts and feelings. Together, they embarked on countless holidays, creating cherished memories and relishing every moment spent in each other's company. Whether hiking through serene mountains, exploring bustling cities, or enjoying quiet evenings by the fire, their companionship was unwavering. Through laughter, tears, triumphs, and tribulations, Neeta and Diana supported each other, their bond becoming unbreakable.

Genuine friends offer unconditional support, honesty, and understanding, standing by you through highs and lows. They celebrate your successes and provide comfort during challenging times. Built on mutual respect, trust, and deep empathy, these friendships are crucial because they offer emotional support, a safe space to share your feelings, and unconditional acceptance, helping you feel valued and accepted for who you are. As we age and life slows down, we realise the importance of having genuine friends.

Over the years, we make many friends, but as our lives change, we often outgrow them or lose touch, especially when distance gets in the way. Most people we call friends are more like acquaintances—we chat and hang out with them casually, but we don't feel comfortable sharing our deepest thoughts and feelings. Sometimes, we'd rather stay home than waste time on superficial friendships. Other times, we socialise to pass the time. The big question for many of us is, "How do I find a true friend at this stage of my life?"

Finding Friendships in Midlife

1. Recognise the Nature of Relationships:

- *Distinguish Between Acquaintances and True Friends*: Reflect on your current relationships and separate those that feel more like surface-level connections from those that offer more resounding emotional support. Focus your energy on nurturing relationships that have the potential to grow into true friendships.

- *Seek Deeper Connections*: Engage in meaningful conversations beyond small talk by sharing your thoughts, experiences, and feelings. Ask open-ended questions that encourage others to open up as well. For instance, instead of just asking about their weekend, ask what they enjoyed the most or what challenges they faced.

- *Move Forward from Relationships that No Longer Serve You*: If someone was once a dear friend and is now letting you down, you may have grown and evolved. It's okay to move forward and seek new friendships that align better with your current needs and values. This can be a challenging but necessary step for personal growth and emotional well-being.

2. Embrace New Opportunities:

- *Be Open to New Experiences*: Keep an open mind and be willing to try new activities. Whether you join a new club, attend a workshop, or travel to a retreat, these experiences can introduce you to people outside your usual social circles.

- *Step Out of Your Comfort Zone*: Challenge yourself to engage in activities that might initially feel intimidating. Attend a social event alone, sign up for a course you've never tried, or participate in a community project. The goal is to meet new people and break out of your routine.

3. Pursue Common Interests:

- *Join Interest-Based Groups*: Identify your hobbies and passions, then find groups or clubs focusing on these activities. For example, if you love hiking, join a local hiking group. If you enjoy reading, join a book club. Shared interests provide a natural foundation for building friendships.

- *Engage in Shared Activities*: Participate actively in group activities. Regular attendance increases the chances of repeatedly interacting with the same people, which helps form bonds. Engage in conversations during these activities to get to know others better.

4. Be Open to Vulnerability:

- *Be Your Authentic Self*: Authenticity fosters trust and deeper connections. Reveal your genuine thoughts and feelings, even if you initially feel uncomfortable. This openness encourages others to reciprocate, creating a more meaningful relationship.

- *Encourage Mutual Sharing*: Opening up about something personal often prompts others to do the same. Listen actively and empathetically to what others share, creating a safe space for mutual vulnerability. This can turn casual acquaintances into close friends.

5. Cultivate Existing Relationships:

- *Strengthen Current Connections*: Reconnect with friends you may have lost touch with or spend more time with those you are already close to. Arrange regular catchups to maintain and deepen these relationships, whether in person, over the phone, or via video calls.

- *Nurture Emotional Support*: Be a dependable friend who offers support during good times and challenges. Celebrate your friends' successes, lend a listening ear when they need to talk and show empathy and understanding. Regularly express gratitude for your friends and their positive impact on your life. Show appreciation through words and actions.

- *Create Cherished Memories*: Plan activities that create lasting memories with your friends. This could be as simple as regular coffee dates, weekend trips, or attending events together. These shared experiences strengthen your bond and create a history of good times.

6. Look for Positive Environments:

- *Seek Uplifting Settings*: Choose environments and activities that promote positivity and well-being. This could include wellness retreats, mindfulness workshops, fitness classes, or volunteer organisations. Positive settings attract people looking to improve their lives and connect with others.

- *Surround Yourself with Enthusiastic People*: Join groups with enthusiastic and supportive members. Their positive energy is contagious and makes it easier to form meaningful connections. Look for welcoming and inclusive communities.

Although having friends is vital for emotional well-being, it's equally crucial to avoid falling into the trap of unhealthy or toxic friendships. The emotional toll of such relationships can be profound, leaving you feeling drained, unsupported, or even diminished. Riding out these relationships requires self-awareness and courage. Recognising when a friendship is causing more harm than good is essential, and having the strength to distance yourself from it is crucial. You foster a more balanced, fulfilling, and resilient life by prioritising connections that nurture and support you. The right friendships are like a sanctuary, while the wrong ones can feel like a storm—challenging to weather and damaging to your inner peace.

FRIENDS

Key Points
1. Genuine friendships offer a sense of belonging and acceptance, crucial for maintaining self-esteem and mental health as one ages and experiences life changes.
2. Identify relationships offering emotional support and deeper connections versus superficial ones. Focus on nurturing these meaningful bonds and moving on from those that no longer align with your values.
3. Open yourself to new experiences and activities, such as joining clubs or attending events, to meet people outside your usual social circles and break your routine.
4. Show your authentic self and encourage mutual sharing to foster deeper connections and trust with others.
5. Reconnect and strengthen current friendships by spending more time together, offering support, and creating lasting memories.

CHILDREN

"Your children are not your children. They are the sons and daughters of Life's longing for itself. They come through you but not from you, and though they are with you, they belong not to you"

- Gibran

The bond a woman shares with her children is profound and unparalleled. Rooted in unconditional love, it encompasses immense joy and purpose. This connection brings out the best in her, teaching patience, empathy, and resilience, which shapes her identity and purpose. While she lays a solid foundation, she understands that her child is not hers to own but a unique individual with their own path. Her heart swells with pride as she watches them explore the world, fostering their independence and celebrating their distinct identity. She unconditionally offers love, supporting their dreams without imposing her own and finding joy in their journey towards self-discovery. This emotional bond underscores the profound significance of a mother's presence, shaping her child's life with love, strength, and an enduring sense of freedom.

In middle age, a woman might be raising a young child, dealing with a teenager's ups and downs, or supporting an adult child finding their way. Each stage brings a mix of joys and struggles. Whether it's the energy of a young child, the turmoil of adolescence, or the new dynamics of adult children, every phase demands patience, love, and strength. As she addresses these challenges, her heart is tested and enriched, reflecting the depth of her commitment and the evolving nature of her role as a mother.

YOUNG CHILDREN

Having my son in my late twenties made me feel mature and ready for the responsibility, and I truly enjoyed it. However, the constant pressure to have a second child overwhelmed me. The thought of another pregnancy in my mid-thirties and the demands of raising a child alone in a nuclear setup felt exhausting. I didn't have the energy I once had and balancing it all seemed unmanageable. In today's world, an increasing number of women choose to have children later in life, often due to the demands of their careers or a desire to enjoy their personal lives before starting a family. As a result, many middle-aged women are finding themselves raising young children. While this can be a time of great personal fulfilment, as they are more mature and their relationships are often well-established, it also brings unique challenges.

As women enter middle age, their bodies change, and they may not have the same energy reserves they once did. The physical demands of parenting a young child can become overwhelming when faced with these biological shifts. Additionally, their parents, who might have been a source of support and caregiving in earlier years, are now ageing and less able to help out. This adds an extra layer of difficulty as these older parents struggle with their own health and mobility issues.

Compounding these challenges, when women reach retirement age, their children may still be finding their footing in life, whether in their careers or personal lives. This ongoing responsibility can burden the parents, who may have hoped to enjoy their retirement years with fewer responsibilities. Balancing the needs of young children with the realities of ageing and evolving family dynamics makes this period particularly complex and challenging.

Middle-aged women faced with the task of raising young children while dealing with the issues mentioned above can adopt several strategies to help them cope:

Prioritise Self-Care and Build Support Networks:

Caring for yourself is vital when raising young children; building a support network enhances this care. Regular exercise, such as daily walks, helps recharge and offers moments of calm. A balanced diet fuels your body, and adequate rest is crucial; consider your bedroom a sanctuary for unwinding with a consistent bedtime routine. Managing stress is also essential. Activities you enjoy, like gardening or knitting, can soothe and rejuvenate you.

A strong support network acts as a safety net. Connect with other parents through local groups for shared experiences and advice. Attend community playgroups or workshops and social interaction. Online communities can also offer support and new perspectives. Additionally, leaning on family and friends for help with childcare or chores can provide much-needed relief.

Delegate Responsibilities:

Sharing responsibilities can lighten your load and bring much-needed relief. If you have a partner, work together to divide daily chores, like one of you handling school drop-offs while the other takes on grocery shopping. This teamwork not only balances the load but also reduces stress. Hiring help, such as a babysitter or a housekeeper, can make a huge difference; coming home to a clean house and knowing your child is well cared for can be incredibly comforting. Additionally, exploring community resources, like after-school programs or local daycare centres, offers your child engaging activities while you take some time to rest or catch up on work. Sharing tasks and seeking help allows you to breathe a little easier and enjoy your time with your family.

Communicate Openly:

Clear communication keeps things running smoothly. It starts with discussing your needs and challenges openly with your partner. If you're overwhelmed, a heartfelt conversation can lead to finding practical solutions together. Set honest expectations about what you can handle; if you need help with tasks like evening routines, clearly expressing this need can foster better understanding and support. Regular family check-ins also play a vital role. These meetings provide a space to reassess responsibilities and address concerns before they spiral out of control. You create a supportive environment where everyone's needs are acknowledged and managed by talking openly and regularly.

Setting Realistic Expectations:

Setting realistic expectations can ease frustration and bring a sense of peace. Focus on small, achievable daily goals, like cooking dinner and helping with homework. Embrace the idea that perfection isn't necessary; if dinner isn't gourmet or the house isn't spotless, it's okay. What truly matters is the love and effort you put into your family. Celebrate the small wins, whether completing a project or enjoying a calm family dinner. Recognising and appreciating these moments can lift your spirits and remind you of the positive aspects of your daily life.

Future Planning:

Financial planning for the future can profoundly

reduce uncertainty and provide a sense of control, acting as a crucial safety net for your family's needs. Imagine setting aside money regularly for your child's education or your retirement to build a secure foundation for the years ahead. Creating a detailed budget and saving consistently helps you feel more confident about emergency planning, adding another layer of reassurance. Developing a plan for unforeseen events, such as having a list of trusted contacts who can step in if something unexpected happens, helps you feel more in control. Knowing that you have strategies for emergencies, whether a health issue or another crisis, can alleviate anxiety and make you feel more equipped to handle whatever comes your way. By addressing these aspects of future planning, you create a solid foundation of security that supports you and your family through life's inevitable ups and downs.

TEENAGE CHILDREN

At 42, I was pleased and content with my life. However, everything changed when my child entered his teenage years. Once a loving and sweet kid, he transformed into a whirlwind of unpredictability that bewildered me.

A simple request for a meal now triggered eye rolls that could rival a Broadway performance. Tidying his room turned into debates more heated than any late-night talk show, and comments on his appearance sparked interrogations that would impress even Sherlock Holmes.

Under the scrutiny of his teenage critiques, I questioned my culinary skills and driving prowess. His newfound obsession with skincare turned our bathroom into a chaotic battleground, with my face packs disappearing like elusive phantoms.

Adding to the chaos, his Instagram adventures brought a wave of teenage drama, and just when I thought I'd seen it all, his sudden fascination with the opposite sex flipped my world upside down. I longed for the simpler days of football friends and novels.

Despite it all, his confident proclamations of future greatness and casual "Chill, Mom" responses made me laugh at his sheer audacity. During this turbulent teenage phase, I couldn't help but admire his boldness even as I undertook the challenges of this new chapter in our lives.

But on a serious note, the enigmatic world of teenagers is a time when they embark on a quest to unravel the mysteries of their own identity. They might argue that black is white just for the sheer thrill of it, even if you're innocently pointing out a mountain right in front of them. Meanwhile, Mother Nature seems to be slyly nudging your ever-impatient self to master the art of patience as you pilot this rollercoaster ride called parenthood.

As your teenager weaves new relationships, forges

bonds, and picks up new habits during this phase, it falls upon you, dear parent, to delve into the intricate workings of their minds and bodies. Your role? To offer unwavering support and understanding without the classic parental line of "We went through this too, so why are you behaving like this?"

During the journey of adolescence, teenagers confront a whirlwind of changes that shape their bodies, minds, and identities. For females, the onset of puberty heralds a cascade of hormonal shifts, with estrogen and progesterone orchestrating the development of sexual characteristics and mood regulation. Meanwhile, males experience a surge of testosterone, fuelling assertiveness, competitiveness, and the quest for social status. These hormonal tempests and profound alterations in brain development, particularly in the prefrontal cortex, can lead to erratic behaviour and emotional turbulence. As bodies morph and minds evolve, concerns about body image often loom, affecting self-esteem and social interactions for both genders. It's a time of sexual awakening, where hormones ignite romantic interests and shape behaviours related to dating and relationships. Understanding the complexities of these changes underscores the need for patience and empathy. Adolescents are not merely vessels of hormones but individuals traversing a transformative path towards adulthood. They require understanding and support as they steer through this tumultuous terrain, striving to make sense of their evolving selves amidst the storm of adolescence.

Dealing with a teenager without losing your mind and avoiding conflict involves several strategies:

1. Practice Patience and Understanding:

Teenagers undergo intense changes that can make their behaviour seem erratic. As a mother, your patience and understanding are vital. For instance, if your teen snaps at you over a minor issue, remember they might be dealing with stress from school or social pressures. Instead of reacting with frustration, calmly acknowledge their feelings by saying, "I can see you're upset right now. Do you want to talk about what's bothering you?" This approach shows empathy and helps them feel heard.

2. Maintain Open Communication:

Creating a safe space for communication is crucial. Let your teenager know they can share their thoughts and feelings without fear of criticism. If your teen comes home feeling down about a friend, ask about their day and listen without rushing to offer advice. You might say, "I noticed you seem a bit off today. Do you want to share what happened at school?" This helps them feel supported and valued. Your child might face many issues a new-age teen faces, as mentioned below. Identify them and communicate with them accordingly.

Top New-Age Issues that Teens Face:	
Social Media	Loneliness
Body Shaming	Sexual Exploration

Peer Pressure	Unhealthy Food Indulgence
Bullying (Cyber and Physical)	Substance Abuse
Body Image Issues	Aca-demic Pressure

3. Set Boundaries with Flexibility:

Having rules is important but being flexible shows respect for your teen's growing independence. If your teen wants to stay out later than usual, discuss it with them to find a compromise. For example, you could say, "I understand you want to stay out later. How about we try extending your curfew by an hour this weekend and see how it goes?" This approach balances structure with their need for autonomy.

4. Offer Emotional Support:

Teenagers often face significant stress from various sources. Offering emotional support means acknowledging their struggles and providing reassurance. If your teen is anxious about an exam, let them know you're there for them. You might say, "I know you're worried about your test. How about we go over some of the material together? You've got this!" This shows that you're invested in their success and well-being.

5. Encourage Independence:

Supporting your teen's independence helps build their confidence. Allow them to make decisions and take on responsibilities, even if they make mistakes. For instance, if your teen wants to manage their allowance, let them handle their money and learn from their choices. You could say, "I'm proud of you for taking charge of your allowance. If you need any advice or run into problems, I'm here to help." This fosters their sense of responsibility and self-reliance.

6. Be a Role Model:

Your behaviour greatly influences your teenager. By managing stress and challenges calmly, you demonstrate how to handle difficulties. If you're dealing with a stressful work deadline, model calm problem-solving by taking deep breaths or making a plan. Letting your teen see you manage stress positively teaches them valuable coping skills.

7. Seek Professional Help if Needed:

Sometimes, professional support is necessary. If your teenager is struggling with serious issues, seeking help from a therapist or counsellor can be beneficial. For example, if your teen shows signs of severe anxiety or depression, consider talking to a mental health professional. You might say, "I've noticed you've been feeling down lately. It might help to talk to someone who can guide us to support you better." This ensures they receive the additional help they might need.

Adolescence is a vulnerable period in which teenagers undergo changes and challenges that can be overwhelming and confusing. They are navigating a phase of life filled with emotional ups and downs, physical transformations, and intense social pressures. Your support can serve as a steady anchor amidst the stormy seas of adolescence, assuring them that they are not alone in their battles.

ADULT CHILDREN

As Aady ventured into adulthood, he found himself tackling a world far different from the comfort of home. Starting college was a milestone he had eagerly anticipated, filled with excitement and anxiety. The initial thrill of stepping into his dream engineering college was tempered by the sadness of being separated from his close-knit circle of friends and family. The prospect of new beginnings and endless opportunities provided some solace, but the emotional weight of farewells lingered.

In the early days, college life seemed like a blissful adventure. Making new friends felt effortless, like swiping right on a dating app, and his primary concerns were choosing which extracurricular activities to dive into and figuring out laundry without turning his whites pink. Armed with homemade goodies from his mother and a wardrobe stocked with fresh clothes, Aady breezed through his initial month in the dorms, savouring the ease of his new environment.

However, the initial euphoria soon gave way to a harsh reality. The illusion of a perfect college experience began to crumble as the pressure of academic expectations mounted. Lectures, assignments, and exams formed an unrelenting cycle of stress that seemed never-ending. Far from the comforting meals he was used to, hostel food only added to his discontent. His once-carefree financial management became a struggle as he spent too much on overpriced restaurant meals, yearning for his mother's cooking.

His once-orderly room deteriorated into a chaotic mess of unwashed clothes and dirty dishes, mirroring the unravelling of his once-idyllic college life. The loneliness of being away from home became starkly apparent when he fell ill. The absence of his parents' nurturing presence was a glaring void, amplifying his feelings of isolation.

Amidst the mounting stress, homesickness, and academic pressure, Aady faced an internal battle that was as daunting as any external challenge. Anxiety and depression gnawed at his peace of mind, threatening to overwhelm him. The relentless pressure to excel compounded his struggles, and he was adrift in a sea of despair.

Aady's journey into adulthood was marked by a profound test of his strength and resilience. The harsh realities of independence replaced the comfort of home and the security of his parents' care. Through the chaos, loneliness, and emotional turmoil, he grappled with the complexities of growing up, learning to carve out his path amidst the trials of a new and demanding chapter in his life.

If your child is a young adult, your role as a mother is far from over. While it may be physically less demanding than when they were younger, it remains mentally exhausting. Supporting them through adult challenges, offering guidance, and being there emotionally requires different energy and commitment. Love and care remain crucial as they contend with new responsibilities and experiences.

Learning Essential Life Skills:

As your child prepares for college and independent living, ensure they learn essential skills like laundry, basic ironing, and handling bed linens. They should be able to cook simple meals, keep their space clean, and manage kitchen and fridge maintenance. These skills are required to maintain a well-organized, hygienic, and self-sufficient living environment, which is crucial for a smooth transition into an independent life.

Regular Check-Ins and Celebrate Small Wins:

Schedule frequent video calls to stay connected and provide a space where your child can openly share their experiences. During these calls, actively listen to their concerns and offer reassurance. Celebrate their achievements, no matter how small, such as finishing a challenging assignment or scoring well on an exam. Send a congratulatory message or a small gift, like a personalised mug, to acknowledge their successes and keep their spirits high. This blend of regular communication and positive reinforcement helps them feel supported and motivated as they navigate their new life.

Visit When Possible:

Always make an effort to visit them when your schedule allows. For example, if they're feeling overwhelmed, plan a weekend visit to spend quality time together, offer a comforting hug, and share a home-cooked meal. Your visit can provide a much-needed break from their routine.

Encourage Independence:

Supporting your child during their transition to adulthood means helping them build the skills and confidence to manage their challenges. Always encourage them to take responsibility for solving their problems while offering guidance when needed. For instance, if they're struggling with a difficult roommate or managing a tight budget, discuss possible solutions with them, but let them take the lead in deciding and implementing the best course of action.

Always support their efforts by acknowledging their decisions and celebrating their successes. If they're trying to balance a heavy course load with a part-time job, help them brainstorm time management strategies and experiment with different approaches to find what works best for them. By encouraging them to tackle their challenges and make their own decisions, you're helping them develop critical life skills and resilience.

For example, if they're facing issues with their academic performance, instead of intervening directly, encourage them to seek help from tutors or academic advisors and guide them in setting up a study plan. By doing so, you're supporting their independence and empowering them to handle future challenges independently. Your role is to be a supportive guide, offering encouragement and advice while allowing them the space to grow and learn from their experiences.

Suggest Professional Help:

If your child shows signs of severe stress or anxiety, gently suggest they seek campus counselling services. For example, if they mention feeling overwhelmed, you could say, "I think it might be helpful to talk to a counsellor. They can offer support and strategies to manage stress." Offer to help by researching counselling options at their college, providing contact information, and even assisting in making an appointment if they're hesitant. Reassure them that seeking help is a positive and proactive step toward well-being and share any personal experiences or stories to normalise the process.

Parents can help young college students overcome challenges, build resilience, and succeed academically and personally by providing support, guidance, and encouragement. Yet, amidst the bittersweet tango of independence and distance, it is imperative for us, as parents, to strike a delicate balance. We must learn to gracefully let our children stumble, fall, and rise again, teaching them to embrace their mistakes and tears as vital parts of their journey to self-discovery. While they may seem invincible in their youthful vigour, they remain vulnerable to pitfalls like addiction, depression, and toxic influences. Hence, it falls upon us to be their unwavering allies, their confidantes in times of turmoil, their safe harbour in a storm of uncertainties.

So, dear parents, not to be disheartened about not being close to your children. Embrace the evolving dynamics with wisdom and grace, knowing that your role as a guiding light transcends mere proximity. Stay vigilant for the telltale signs of struggle, offer a listening ear without judgment, and nurture a bond where your child can seek solace, share their fears, and shed tears amidst a world that may seem indifferent. Let your love shine through the darkest nights, reminding your children that no matter their path, you stand steadfast by their side, ready to catch them when they fall and embrace them when they need to be held like a child again.

Empty Nest Syndrome:

Life takes us on unexpected journeys, and one of the most defining moments is when our children spread their wings and leave the nest that we once called home. The sound of laughter, arguments, and occasional tantrums fade into the hollow silence that seeps through empty rooms. This phenomenon, known as empty nest syndrome, leaves parents waving goodbye to their role as the resident "shouters-in-chief" and losing their partners-in-blame.

Amidst the bittersweet emotions, however, lies a golden opportunity for personal growth, reinvention, and a dynamic shift. It's a journey filled with raw emotions of missing someone to shower with love, spoil with limitless affection, and engage in life's most absurd yet endearing moments.

Remembering the wisdom of our ancestors, who had bustling households and built-in support systems, we realise that modern families often face this transition alone. We miss our children's laughter, feel the pain of their absence, and are touched by well-meaning friends' jokes about the empty nest syndrome. Yet, we sail across this sea of emotions with vulnerability and strength, shedding tears over songs that remind us of family road trips or when stumbling upon childhood drawings.

As time passes, solace is found in the bond with our child. Shared memories fuel us as we embrace the quiet and rediscover neglected hobbies and self-care. Excitement grows for our child's growth and transformation. As they embark on a new chapter, we prepare for this empty nest syndrome by cherishing freedom, finding new companions, reclaiming passions, and embracing adventures with optimism and love.

Key Points:

1. Middle-aged women raising young children face challenges such as decreased energy accompanying ageing and limited parental support for raising children as they face health issues. To cope, they should prioritise self-care, build support networks, delegate responsibilities, communicate openly and set realistic expectations.

2. Adolescence requires patience and empathy as teens face intense hormonal changes, mood swings, and social pressures. This is the time for open communication, setting flexible boundaries, and offering emotional support to your teenage child. If necessary, seek professional help to address serious issues, ensuring your teen feels supported through their transformative years.

3. Supporting young adults involves guiding them through life by teaching them life skills, encouraging their independence, and allowing them to grow; however, they still require your support when life takes them on unpredictable journeys. Therefore, keep your channels of communication open and, if they are living separately, visit them often.

4. Empty nest syndrome, though filled with the bittersweet pain of a child's departure, offers a golden opportunity for personal growth, reinvention, and rediscovering passions as parents embrace their newfound freedom and continue to cherish their evolving bond with their child.

AGEING PARENTS

In the quiet corners of their spacious Lucknow bungalow, Gopal and Shanti Das shared a life intertwined with memories of love, sacrifice, and the unbreakable bond of family. But as the years rolled by, their once-vibrant home began to echo with the emptiness of solitude.

Now in his twilight years, Gopal grappled with a sense of isolation that seemed to deepen with each passing day. The comforting routines of his retired life no longer held the same warmth without the familiar laughter of friends and the bustling presence of loved ones. Despite the comfort of a pension that provided for their needs, Gopal couldn't shake off the gnawing feeling of irrelevance that crept into his heart.

Shanti, his ever-resilient partner, continued to be the steadfast anchor of their household. With each sunrise, she seamlessly juggled the responsibilities of the home, her quiet strength a beacon of unwavering support for her husband. Yet, beneath her composed exterior, Shanti harboured her silent ache—the longing for the laughter of grandchildren and the tender embrace of children who had ventured far from their childhood home.

As the clock ticked towards 11 am, the anticipation in the air was palpable. Gopal and Shanti would sit side by side on the sofa, their hearts yearning for the daily video call that bridged the physical distance between them and their scattered family.

"Do you think they'll call today, Shanti?" Gopal's voice was tinged with hope as he glanced at the silent phone, his fingers tapping against the armrest.

Shanti smiled softly, her eyes reflecting the same longing in her husband's heart. "I'm sure they will, Gopal. They always do."

But the screen remained blank.

Gopal Das suffers from loneliness and wants a little time from his children. There are times when parents need more than just time—they may be sick and need your care, or they might need financial assistance, especially in India, where they often spend all their money securing their children's future instead of their own. Caring for them isn't a duty; it's a legacy we pass on to our children. How we treat our elders reflects the accurate measure of our society and the love we hope to leave behind.

Amidst the burden of life's obligations, it's easy to lose sight of the ones who've been our pillars from the start—our ageing parents. As we rush through our days, juggling work, family, and the ever-growing to-do list, the care of our parents often becomes an item on the checklist rather than a priority. Yet, as the years pass and our children sprout wings, a haunting realisation dawns upon us—the guilt of not being there for our parents when they needed us most. We often overlook the countless things our parents have done for us, focusing instead on the few things they couldn't do. We fail to see their loneliness and their longing for love.

But amidst the chaos, there lies a ray of hope—a roadmap to reconnecting with our beloved. As we live in nuclear families away from our parents, it can be challenging to be present in their lives as much as we would like. However, the following ways deepen the bond and ensure they feel loved.

Regular Communication:

Even amidst a busy schedule, setting aside 5 to 10 minutes for a phone call with your parents can be incredibly meaningful. This small gesture allows you to listen to Dad recount stories from his past or hear Mom reminisce about old times. These brief moments of connection offer a comforting break from daily stress and show that you care, helping to maintain a solid emotional attachment despite physical distance.

Quality Time Together:

Coordinating family visits might feel overwhelming, but the joy of spending time together is invaluable. The shared laughter, heartfelt conversations, and moments like watching Dad try to master a new technology or Mom experiment with a new recipe can create lasting memories. Though seemingly small, these activities foster a deeper connection and provide you and your parents with treasured experiences.

Practical Help:

Helping with everyday tasks, such as household chores or errands, may not seem glamorous, but it is precious. This practical support alleviates some of their daily burdens and shows solidarity and care. The relief and gratitude you see on their faces when you lend a hand can be a profound reminder of the impact of your support.

Show Empathy:

Listening to your parents' concerns, fears, and joys with genuine compassion creates a space for authentic connection. Acknowledging their emotions and offering comfort helps validate their experiences and strengthens your relationship. This empathetic approach fosters a deeper understanding and builds a solid foundation of love and support.

Through communication, quality time, practical help, or compassion, these efforts form the cornerstone of a loving relationship with your ageing parents. Embracing these moments enriches their lives and yours, making each interaction a cherished part of your shared journey.

CARING FOR AILING PARENTS

Caring for our ailing parents is a journey that delves deep into the rest of our hearts, stirring emotions we never knew existed. As we witness the gradual decline of once-robust figures who raised us with strength and love, it feels like a piece of our childhood slipping away. The weight of their dependence on us, both emotionally and physically, is like an anchor securing us to an ocean of mixed emotions—love, sadness, and exhaustion intertwine in a bittersweet symphony of caregiving. Taking care of ailing parents without feeling overwhelmed involves balancing their needs and your well-being. By embracing these steps, you can provide compassionate care while nurturing your resilience and peace of mind.

Balancing Empathy and Efficiency:

Spearheading the role of a caregiver requires balancing empathy with efficiency. This means offering emotional support while managing the practical aspects of care. For example, when a parent is anxious about a new treatment, it's essential to provide reassurance and comfort while organising medical appointments and handling prescriptions. This ensures that their emotional needs are met alongside their practical requirements, creating a holistic approach to caregiving.

Effective Communication:

Communication is vital in caregiving, helping to coordinate efforts and share responsibilities. Regular updates and discussions with family members and fellow caregivers can alleviate the burden on any one person. For instance, setting up a shared family calendar or group chat to track appointments, medication schedules, and care plans ensures everyone is on the same page and can contribute effectively to the care process.

Honouring Autonomy and Dignity:

Respecting your parents' autonomy is crucial in maintaining their dignity as they grapple with vulnerability. Involving them in decisions about their health care and respecting their preferences, even when they differ from your choice, helps them retain a sense of control and self-worth. For example, asking them their opinion on treatment options or letting them choose their daily routines ensures they feel valued and empowered.

Continuous Learning:

Staying informed about your parents' medical conditions and treatment options is essential for effective caregiving. Continuous learning involves researching their health issues, attending medical appointments, and seeking reliable resources and support groups. Understanding the specifics of their condition and potential treatments allows you to advocate for the best possible care and make informed decisions about their health management.

Seeking Professional Support:

When caregiving becomes overwhelming, seeking professional help is a crucial step. This could mean hiring a home health aide, consulting with a counsellor, or joining a caregiver support group. Professional support provides relief and ensures you and your parents receive the care and guidance needed. For example, a professional caregiver can take over some daily tasks, giving you a much-needed break and helping you manage stress effectively.

Prioritising Self-Care:

Taking care of your well-being is essential for sustaining your caregiving efforts. Self-care involves setting aside time for yourself, seeking support from loved ones, and engaging in activities that rejuvenate you. For example, scheduling regular exercise, enjoying a hobby, or simply relaxing helps maintain your physical, mental, and emotional health. By prioritising self-care, you ensure you have the resilience and energy to provide ongoing, compassionate care for your parents.

Integrating these practices into your caregiving routine helps create a balanced, supportive environment that honours your parents' needs and your well-being.

MENDING FENCES

Navigating Strained Relationships with Parents

Rita's childhood was a turbulent stream marred by her father's emotional abuse, its currents carrying the weight of relentless criticism and belittlement. Each day dawned with dread as harsh words and cold silence shaped her world. Childhood, for Rita, bore the scars of a wounded soul yearning for healing.

Some individuals have a childhood filled with warmth, love, and stability. However, others walk a more challenging path, where financial struggles, conflicts within the family unit, or even the harsh reality of abuse cast long shadows over their formative years, creating stormy weather in their childhood memories. As children, we may lack the maturity and understanding to comprehend the circumstances that shape our upbringing entirely. It's common to assign blame and resentment to our parents, whom we perceive as the source of our struggles. However, as we grow older and gain perspective, we begin to see our caregivers not just as authority figures but as flawed individuals who carry their burdens and imperfections.

Rita's past loomed over her present like a persistent storm cloud, casting a shadow that darkened her every moment with self-doubt and fear. The wounds of her childhood abuse seeped into her daily life, poisoning her relationships and work with a toxic blend of insecurity and anxiety. Each interaction carried the weight of past pain, leaving Rita trapped in a cycle of doubt and mistrust. The memories of her abusive parent's voice haunted her, chipping away at her confidence and sense of self-worth, creating a barrier between Rita and the peace she longed for.

If you have a turbulent past with a parent like Rita did, finding peace is crucial but often challenging because we naturally try to avoid pain and hurt. The following steps will help make this journey a little easier.

Confronting Pain and Legacy:

Traversing the complexities of a problematic past requires immense courage and introspection. It involves facing the pain we carry within ourselves, often a legacy passed down through generations. For instance, if a family has a history of unresolved conflicts or emotional trauma, addressing these issues means confronting the lingering hurt that has affected multiple generations. This can be an intensely emotional process, requiring acknowledging and working through the pain inherited or compounded over time.

Seeking Support:

Addressing these deep-seated wounds, whether through honest conversations with our parents or with the help of a trained therapist, is like unravelling a tightly knotted rope. Engaging in open dialogue with family members can be challenging but is essential for understanding and healing. For example, having a heartfelt conversation with a parent about past grievances or seeking therapy can provide a safe space to explore and process these emotions. Although this work can be draining, it is crucial for achieving peace and personal healing.

Embracing Forgiveness:

Forgiveness can be a powerful balm for the soul

in the journey towards reconciliation. While addressing past hurts can be difficult, it offers a chance to transform emotional scars into stories of resilience, strength, and hope. For instance, forgiving a parent for past mistakes allows you to release long-held anger and resentment, which can lead to personal growth and emotional freedom. This process helps reshape painful memories into valuable lessons and sources of strength.

Valuing Time with Loved Ones:

Time is a fleeting companion, leaving us uncertain about how many moments we have spent with those who raised us. This reminder underscores the importance of cherishing our time with loved ones and maximising every opportunity to connect and heal. For example, prioritising time with ageing parents or mending relationships can ensure we create lasting, meaningful memories before it's too late.

So, if you're fortunate to have your parents by your side still, take a moment to hold their hands a little tighter, listen to their stories a little more intently, and express your gratitude for the unspoken sacrifices made along the way. Our parents are the threads that weave our stories together, painting a portrait of love, resilience, and unwavering support. In life's grand story, standing by your parents and completing the circle of existence is a rare privilege. Embrace this blessing, cherish their love, and hold dear the timeless connection shared.

Key Points

1. Witnessing our parents' ageing as we age isn't easy. The best way to show our love to them is to offer them quality time, empathy, and practical help while keeping communication channels open.

2. Caring for ailing parents involves planning and efficiency. It's crucial to maintain open communication with family and caregivers and respect your parents' dignity by honouring their preferences. Seeking professional help and prioritising self-care is essential to managing the emotional and physical demands of caregiving while ensuring your well-being and theirs.

3. Healing from turbulent relationships with your parents is a complex process but essential. It requires you to confront deep-seated pain with your parents and a therapist. Healing is a long and continuous process that can only come when we acknowledge our pain and forgive the person involved to honour the bond of love and legacy.

SIBLINGS

I am the youngest in the family, with two elder sisters who spoiled me rotten. Despite being mature, I was always protected by them. We had endless fights over clothes, food, comics, and TV—we could argue about anything. But as we grew older, we became closer and became best friends and confidants. After marriage and starting our own families, we got busy and self-centred. Though we remained siblings, we somehow lost our deep friendship.

Yet, something still binds us together. We can't stand to see each other in pain, no matter how angry we get. We shout and fight, but in the end, we care deeply and always look out for each other. Siblings are the closest you can ever be to someone genetically, apart from parents and children. There is something in this bond that keeps us together no matter what. We fight, forgive, and forget, but we can never stay away from each other.

Siblings become even more valuable as we reach middle age. They offer emotional support that is hard to find elsewhere because they've known us our whole lives. The memories we share with them are like a comforting bridge to our past, helping us meet the changes and challenges that come with midlife. They understand our quirks and personality traits better than anyone, offering a sense of acceptance and empathy that is truly unique.

One of the greatest advantages of having a sibling is their ability to give you honest advice without worrying about your reaction. They know you inside out and aren't afraid to tell you the truth, even if it's hard to hear. This honesty, rooted in love and understanding, helps to guide you through life's challenges. Their candid words, delivered with care, can offer clarity and support like no one else can, making the sibling bond incredibly special and invaluable.

The biggest challenge with siblings often lies in competing for the same resources—whether it's our parents' love, attention, or approval. Growing up, it's easy to feel like there isn't enough to go around, leading to conflicts and rivalry. These struggles can stir up deep emotions, making us feel like we're constantly vying for a place in our parents' hearts. Yet, beneath these conflicts is a shared bond, and understanding that these fights are a natural part of sibling dynamics can help us negotiate and eventually strengthen our relationships.

As we grow older, sibling rivalry can sometimes turn ugly, but it's up to us to prioritise our relationships over material possessions. With time, our number of close relationships dwindle, and siblings often become some of our most enduring bonds. No amount of wealth or worldly belongings can replace the love and connection we share with them. Choosing to nurture and value this bond above all else reminds us that the true wealth in life lies in the relationships we cherish.

Strengthening bonds with siblings in middle age is essential and can be deeply fulfilling. Here are some ways to enhance these relationships:

Resolve Conflicts:

Addressing past conflicts or misunderstandings with your siblings can be challenging, but it's essential for building a stronger relationship. Begin by approaching the conversation with patience and an open mind. Understand that you may have different perspectives and feelings about the situation. Express your thoughts and emotions honestly, but also be open to listening to your sibling's side of the story. Acknowledging past hurts and validating each other's feelings can help heal old wounds. It's essential to focus on resolving the issue rather than assigning blame. Look for common ground and work together to find a solution that feels fair to both of you.

Celebrating Each Other's Milestones:

Celebrating each other's milestones and achievements is a powerful way to strengthen the bond with your siblings. These moments of recognition and joy create a positive and supportive atmosphere in your relationship. Whether it's a birthday, a work promotion, a personal accomplishment, or even a small victory, acknowledging these moments shows that you care about each other's happiness and success. Showing genuine interest in your sibling's achievements fosters a sense of pride and mutual respect. It reminds both of you that you are valued and appreciated. This positive reinforcement can help build a foundation of support and encouragement, making your relationship more resilient and loving.

Supporting Each Other in Times of Need:

Supporting each other in need is fundamental to building and maintaining strong sibling bonds, particularly as we enter middle age. Life inevitably throws challenges our way, and having a sibling to lean on can make a significant difference in how we deal with these trials.

When one sibling faces a difficult situation, be it a health issue, a career setback, or a personal loss, the other can provide invaluable support. This support can take many forms, from offering a listening ear to giving practical help. For example, if your sibling is going through a divorce, simply being there to listen and provide emotional support can be incredibly comforting. Helping with daily tasks, like cooking a meal or caring for their children, can alleviate some of their burden.

In times of need, it's not just about being present physically but also emotionally. Showing genuine concern, understanding their struggles, and offering encouragement can help them feel less alone and more hopeful. Sometimes, just knowing that someone cares deeply can provide the strength to overcome adversity.

Additionally, supporting each other in times of need fosters a sense of mutual trust and reliance. It reinforces the idea that you have someone who will stand by your side no matter what happens. This sense of security can be exceptionally comforting as we age, knowing that there is always someone there for us, just as we are there for them.

Supporting each other also involves celebrating successes and joys. Being there for your sibling during happy times, like promotions, anniversaries, or the birth of a child, strengthens the bond and creates shared memories that bring you closer together.

Fostering Deep Connections with Siblings Through Shared Activities and Memories:

Engaging in shared activities, organising regular family gatherings, reminiscing about childhood memories, and planning trips together can significantly strengthen your bond with siblings during middle age. Organising simple family dinners or weekend visits keeps the family spirit alive and provides opportunities to share meals and conversations, fostering a sense of unity. Additionally, taking time to reminisce about your childhood and sharing stories or looking at old photos can bring a sense of nostalgia and reinforce the unique bond you share. Planning a sibling trip to explore new places can be a fantastic way to bond and create lasting memories. Combining these activities nurtures a deeper connection and strengthens your relationship with your siblings.

EXTENDED FAMILY

I come from a sprawling extended family—my mother has three siblings, and my father has seven, making it hard to count all my cousins. Compared to my son, who has just four cousins, my childhood summers in our hometown in Kumaon were vibrant and full of people. Each year, our house would come alive with the energy of three generations under one roof: wise grandparents, strict parents, and adventurous cousins. Those summer vacations were filled with unforgettable escapades—sneaking out to buy samosas, walking ten kilometres for a piece of cake, climbing trees to steal mangoes, and saving each other from trouble while getting our fair share of punishments. Those two months were a golden period when we lived fully, and even our parents eased up on the pressure of studies. It was a time of joy and endless adventures that I hold close to my heart.

I often wondered what glued us together– was it our shared bloodline, the values we followed, or the culture we grew up in? I realised it's a mix of all these things. As time passed, we all got busy with our careers and families and somehow lost touch with each other. We still met occasionally at weddings, but it wasn't the same. As we age and our responsibilities lessen, there's a sudden urge to reconnect with our childhood and relive those fond memories. The desire to revisit those joyful times and strengthen the bonds we once had grows stronger, reminding us of the precious moments we shared. Even now, our minds flood with childhood memories when we meet them. Despite most of us being over 50, we feel like children again whenever we're together. It's crucial to rekindle these relationships during middle age, as they connect us to our ancestors. Although there are sometimes family feuds and unmet expectations between cousins, making peace as we age is essential. These connections are unique in our hearts, offering comfort and a sense of belonging deeply rooted in our shared past.

Relationships require effort and positivity to thrive. Investing positive energy into your connections often returns to you meaningfully, even if not directly from the person you're focusing on. Your children might observe and absorb this positivity, applying it to their lives. Strive to avoid conflicts with loved ones, as disputes can be deeply painful. If a relationship becomes toxic, it's better to step away rather than engage in constant fighting. In the end, conflicts can sever bonds and leave bitterness behind. Remember, where there is love, there can be hurt, but maintaining a loving and positive approach helps preserve these meaningful connections and fosters a healthier, more supportive environment for everyone involved.

SIBLINGS

Key Points:

1. Siblings offer unique emotional support and honest advice, deeply understanding each other's personalities. Resolve conflicts, celebrate milestones, and support each other to strengthen these invaluable relationships

2. Cherish Extended Family: Rekindling connections with extended family, including cousins, can provide comfort and a sense of belonging. Shared memories from childhood offer a strong foundation for renewing bonds and reconnecting.

Part Three
Rediscovering Yourself

INTRODUCTION

Midlife transformation is not a sudden event but a gradual process like a slow sunrise, where the light of change gradually brightens the horizon. For a woman, it's not just about the physical alterations but a deep stirring of emotions and a quest for spiritual growth. What used to feel merely ordinary now seems achingly mundane, and she yearns for something more that aligns with her soul's depths. This is a time for self-discovery, a journey inward to understand and embrace the true self.

In this journey, she discovers the value of her time and energy, no longer willing to squander it on shallow connections or meaningless pursuits. Instead, she craves depth and authenticity in her relationships. She's done with carrying the weight of anger and resentment, and boundaries become her armour, empowering her to shield her tender heart from harm as she bravely and determinedly ventures forth for a purpose.

During this time, a woman often finds herself at a crossroads, questioning her assumed roles and identities. She begins to explore what defines her beyond the labels of mother, wife, or professional. Amidst this transformation, many women find solace and guidance in their faith or spirituality, which becomes a significant and comforting part of their journey.

In this transformative journey, she learns that midlife is not an end but a new beginning. This realisation fills her with hope and optimism, as she knows she can liberate herself, redefine herself, pursue her passions, and live a life reflecting her inner light. Through this process, she emerges stronger, wiser, and more connected to her true self, ready to embrace the future with open arms and a heart full of hope.

Discovering Your
IDENTITY

Shobha, a simple, educated girl, always dreamt of making a name for herself. After completing her post-graduate studies, her parents insisted she marry before starting her career. She entered into marriage with little choice and feeling the weight of societal expectations. Unaware of the big changes it would bring, this new life swept her away from her present identity. The first significant change came when her new family decided on her surname without consulting her. Overnight, her identity shifted from Shobha to Mrs. Shobha Roy, Rajat Roy's wife. The decision was made for her, and her name was changed in all her documents, stripping away a piece of her individuality.

As time passed, the family's focus remained on her role within the household, particularly in taking care of the family and raising children. When Shanti was born 1.5 years later, she became Shanti's mother, further losing herself in the roles assigned to her by others. She was no longer just Shobha; she was Rajat's wife, Shanti's mother, Mrs. Shobha Roy. Her dreams of working and creating her identity faded into the background as her family showed little interest in supporting her aspirations, prioritising their comfort over her fulfilment.

Despite trying her hand at various jobs, the lack of support made it difficult for her to succeed. She slowly made peace with her life, that she could have a job but not a flourishing career. She accepted her role in the household and buried her dreams deep within her heart. One day, when her teenage daughter, with innocent curiosity, asked, "Mummy, what do you do all day? You don't have your own identity," her peace was shattered.

Her words pierced Shobha like a sharp blade, cutting through the layers of resignation she had built over the years. At that moment, she realised how much she had sacrificed her dreams and identity to fulfil everyone else's needs. Her central focus had become ensuring those around her had all they needed to flourish, and in the process, she had lost herself. The emotional weight of this realisation was overwhelming, bringing tears to her eyes as she reflected on her life and the person she had become.

Shobha's story reflects today's Indian society, where such narratives are so familiar and accepted that they often seem mundane and unremarkable. Many women find their dreams and identities submerged under the weight of familial expectations and societal norms. This silent, pervasive reality remains unchallenged, making stories like Shobha's all too familiar, though things are beginning to change.

Despite having a good husband, healthy children, and a comfortable life, Shobha was unhappy because she had lost touch with herself. Her identity had become solely defined by her roles as a wife and mother, leaving little room for her aspirations, interests, and dreams. This lack of personal identity left her empty and unable to express her true self. When her daughter innocently questioned her about her identity, it struck a deep chord within Shobha. It reminded her of the dreams she had set aside and the parts of herself she had buried to fulfil others' expectations, and this moment brought into sharp focus the disconnect between who she had become and who she wanted to be, stirring an emotional realisation of her own unmet needs and desires.

Recognising your identity means genuinely understanding who you are—your beliefs, strengths, and values—and staying true to yourself. It's about being authentic and consistent in your actions and thoughts, embracing your flaws, and making decisions based on your values rather than external pressures.

Losing one's identity in a relationship extends beyond compromising on a career; it deeply creeps into emotional, social, and personal well-being. The slow erosion of self-worth happens as the woman constantly seeks validation from her partner, gradually neglecting their own feelings and desires in favour of those of their spouse and children. Painful isolation from friends and family occurs, with once-cherished supportive networks fading away. There is the quiet abandonment of hobbies that once brought joy. Individual choices are conceded, and dependence on the partner's decisions erodes independence. Heart-wrenching conformity to the partner's identity leads to suppressing one's authentic self to fit into the relationship mould. Personal goals are abandoned, and dreams that once fuelled their spirit lie dormant. With time, women watch themselves as they become a fading reflection of who they were.

Rediscovering your identity is about finding your way back to yourself. It's about honouring your dreams, passions, and values and allowing them to shine in every aspect of your life.

Reclaiming Your Identity in a Relationship.

1. Reflect on What Truly Matters:

Look inward to understand your beliefs, values, and dreams. This self-reflection helps you reconnect with what truly matters to you. For example, if you used to love painting but haven't touched a brush in years, now is the time to set up a small art corner at home and start creating again. Revisiting these passions can reignite a sense of joy and fulfilment that may have been overshadowed by your roles as a partner and parent.

2. Communicate Openly with Your Partner:

Engage in open and honest communication with your partner. Share your feelings and explain why having personal space and time for your interests is essential for your well-being. For instance, you might explain how attending a weekly yoga class helps you feel centred and rejuvenated, making you happier and more content. By expressing your needs clearly, you can work together to create a balance that allows you to thrive individually and as a couple.

3. Pursue Personal and Career Goals:

Reignite your purpose and fulfilment by identifying important aspirations, such as starting a garden, learning a new language, or training for a 5K run. Career goals are equally important; consider advancing your skills through professional courses, seeking a promotion, or even changing career paths if they align with your passions. For instance, learning coding can significantly upskill you in today's tech-driven world, opening new career opportunities and boosting your confidence. Investing time in self-improvement enhances your skills and self-esteem.

4. Nurture Friendships Outside Your Relationship:

Maintaining friendships outside of your relationship provides additional support and different perspectives. Spend time with friends who uplift you and remind you of who you are as an individual. For instance, a coffee date with a close friend can offer new perspectives and much-needed laughter, breaking the routine of daily life. Stay in touch with old friends and try to form new connections to enrich your social life and maintain a balanced perspective.

5. Celebrate Your Individuality:

Celebrate your big and small achievements. Completing a book that you've been meaning to read or mastering a new recipe are achievements worth celebrating. Find creative outlets to express yourself, such as starting a personal blog, creating a photo album of your adventures, or engaging in any passion that reverberates with you. Embracing and celebrating your uniqueness, like organising a small exhibit of your artwork for friends and family, will empower you to live authentically and enjoy the journey of rediscovering yourself.

When Shobha's husband Rajat saw his wife simply fading away over time with no desires, expectations, or dreams, he realised his wife was not happy. For years together, he always believed he could make her happy by giving her a comfortable life. How wrong he was, he realised as he saw her lifeless figure going through the daily routine like a robot. A heartfelt conversation with Shobha made him think about the real Shobha; the girl who once had big dreams of making a name for herself. She had now become Mrs Rajat Roy with no dreams or aspirations.

After this moment of realisation, everything changed for Shobha. Rajat and her daughter became her biggest cheerleaders and started a YouTube channel for her that demonstrated her cooking skills. With the help of her husband's software skills and her talent, the channel flourished, and so did she. Now she has many admirers, some of whom are now her friends, including her husband, who is sometimes addressed as Shobha's husband now. Ah! The irony of life!

This journey is a chance for Shobha to reclaim her essence, stand tall in her authenticity, and live a true life. Rediscovering one's identity is a deeply personal and transformative process. It requires support, courage, introspection, and a willingness to embrace change. But the rewards are immeasurable for Shobha and any woman on this path.

Reclaiming your identity is about rediscovering and embracing who you are beyond your roles as per societal norms. It's a journey that empowers you to live authentically, find joy in being yourself, and maintain a healthy balance between your personal and shared life.

Before losing yourself in a relationship, remember that there is only one you in this world with your unique dreams, aspirations, and interests. You must prioritise your journey and leave a legacy to avoid losing the essence of who you are. Embrace your individuality, pursue your passions, and nurture your personal growth alongside your relationship, ensuring your life reflects your authentic self. This way, you can build a fulfilling future where your presence in the world leaves a meaningful and lasting impact.

Educated Homemakers: A new social class

According to World Bank data, although women constitute 48% of India's population, they have not benefitted equally from the country's economic growth. India has among the lowest female labour force participation rates globally, with fewer than a third of women aged 15 and older working or actively seeking employment. Indian women have been attending schools and universities like never before, yet the percentage of women in the workforce has decreased over time. Surveys indicate that the rising education levels of women are often driven by marriage. Families and sons increasingly seek educated daughters-in-law, not for their earning potential, but to ensure the next generation is highly educated. This trend has given rise to a new social class: educated homemakers. These women, equipped with advanced degrees and skills, are expected to prioritise family duties over personal ambitions, often leading to unexpressed frustrations and unfulfilled aspirations.

They are skilled in thinking strategically and leading, yet their domain is confined to the four walls of the home. Empowered with knowledge and capabilities, they nurture their children's and families' minds while their aspirations take a back seat. This dichotomy can lead to a well of unspoken frustrations and unfulfilled dreams bubbling beneath the surface, waiting to erupt. A significant cause of anger and frustration among these educated homemakers remains unresolved, as blame is often shifted between the girls' parents, the husbands, and the women themselves. However, a deeper examination reveals that systemic changes in societal structures could alleviate these tensions. By creating more job opportunities that offer flexible working hours, establishing safe and affordable childcare facilities, and promoting the equitable sharing of household responsibilities between men and women, we can pave the way for more women to enter and thrive in the workforce.

In India, the lack of safe spaces for young children poses a significant challenge for working women. Caring for children often falls on grandparents, particularly grandmothers, who step in to fill the gap. While grandparents may cherish the time spent with their grandchildren, the burden of childcare can be overwhelming and restrict their freedom and personal pursuits. It is essential to recognise that childcare is a collective responsibility that should be shared among family members and not disproportionately shouldered by any individual.

Always remember, just as an educated woman can raise educated children, so too can an educated, frustrated, and angry woman unwittingly transfer her trauma to the next generation. Her influence is immense; her emotional state can shape the lives of those around her, traversing through time. Let us be mindful of the legacy we leave, striving to instil future generations with strength, resilience, and hope.

Key Points
1. Many women's identities become overshadowed by familial roles and societal expectations. Losing oneself in these roles can lead to discontent and emptiness, diminishing one's sense of worth.
2. Finding your identity is a journey you must embark on if you want to grow beyond societal expectations. It involves communicating your needs with loved ones and identifying your passion.
3. Having a circle of friends and hobbies separate from your immediate family will help you gain a different perspective on life and reconnect you with your authentic self.
4. The rise of educated homemakers in India reflects a trend where women with advanced degrees are expected to prioritise family duties over personal ambitions. This disparity often leads to unfulfilled aspirations and frustration. Addressing systemic issues such as flexible job opportunities, childcare support, and shared household responsibilities can help bridge this gap and enable women to thrive both personally and professionally.

Setting
BOUNDARIES

*N*ita was a whirlwind of energy. She would always rush in to save the day with her boundless kindness and generosity, though her habit of giving without limits was hard to understand. She was always the first to volunteer, whether helping at a community event or supporting a friend in need.

Nita was a devoted wife, loving mother, and hardworking employee. Her days were packed with school runs, tuition classes, endless PTA meetings, and office work pressure. Her reputation for selflessness exceeded her friendships; it touched every part of her family life. She was the queen of multitasking, able to whip up dinner, help with homework, and settle sibling squabbles simultaneously. Her friends often admired how she could conjure snacks out of thin air and find lost toys with just a glance.

Despite her status, Nita's reluctance to set boundaries began to strain her relationships at home and work. She said yes to every request, every demand, and every tiny whim of her husband, children, friends, and coworkers. Her days were blurred together by *many obligations, leaving her little time for herself and her needs.*

Even with the joy from her wonderful husband, loving children, and supportive friends, Nita's struggle with setting boundaries led to frustration. Constantly putting others' needs before her own, she found herself stretched thin, unable to carve out time for self-care or pursue personal interests. This constant cycle of overextending herself left Nita feeling emotionally drained and unfulfilled as her desires and well-being took a backseat to the demands of others. The internal conflict between her desire to please and the necessity of self-preservation weighed heavily on Nita, highlighting the importance of setting healthy boundaries for her happiness and peace of mind.

Nita was a people-pleaser who found it hard to set boundaries. People-pleasing often originates from deep-seated insecurities and a longing for acceptance that traces back to early life experiences. This behaviour is rooted in the hope of securing a sense of belonging and self-worth by making others happy. Suppose you find it challenging to set boundaries because you think you are a people pleaser with deeper issues. In that case, you must work with a therapist who can identify the real reason behind it and work on you at a deeper level.

Setting boundaries is like establishing personal rules for how you want to be treated by others and how you will interact with the world. It means deciding what behaviour is acceptable and what is not, both in terms of how others treat you and how you treat yourself.

By setting boundaries, you create a framework that helps you navigate relationships and situations in a way that is healthy and respectful to yourself. It's like drawing a line around your emotional, physical, and mental space to protect your well-being and ensure that you are treated with the care and consideration you deserve.

Boundaries also show others how you expect to be treated, setting the tone for mutual respect and understanding in your interactions. They are essential for maintaining balance, self-respect, and healthy relationships, as they help you prioritise your needs and take control of your life.

Setting boundaries can look different depending on the situation. Here are some examples to show how boundaries work in other parts of life:

> **Personal Space**: If a friend or coworker stands too close, you might say, "I feel more comfortable with a bit more distance between us."
>
> **Time**: If your schedule is full and a colleague asks for help, you might say, "I wish I could help, but I have other commitments. Maybe next time."
>
> **Emotional**: If a family member criticises your choices, you could say, "I value your opinion, but constant criticism is not helpful. Let's support each other in positive ways."
>
> **Financial**: If a friend borrows money without returning it, you might say, "I want to help you, but I need to meet my financial obligations. Let's come up with a repayment plan."

In these examples, setting boundaries means clearly and respectfully communicating your needs, preferences, or limits. Boundaries are about caring for yourself and ensuring your relationships and interactions align with your values and well-being.

How to set boundaries?

Self-Reflection and Awareness: Before setting boundaries, take time to understand your own needs and limits. Think about past experiences where your boundaries were crossed and how it made you feel. For example, if you feel uncomfortable when a friend constantly puts you down in front of others, recognise that this is a boundary you must set.

Effective Communication: Set your boundaries by using clear and kind communication. Express your feelings without blaming others by using "I" statements. For instance, you could tell your friend, "I feel uncomfortable when someone puts me down in public. Like, the other day, I felt terrible because of what was said about me in front of everyone."

Specific Boundary Setting: Be specific about what behaviours cross your boundaries and the consequences. Tell your friend, "I need you to stop publicly saying unkind words about me. If you don't, I won't be able to accompany you."

Consistent Enforcement: Stick to your boundaries every time they are challenged. This shows that you are serious about them. If your friend disrespects you again, remind them, "I need to be treated with respect in public. I will leave if my dignity is compromised."

Reciprocal Respect: Respect others' boundaries too. If your friend tells you they need their space or time, honour that request. This mutual respect strengthens your relationship. For example, if your friend says they need time alone, give them that space without questioning it.

Seeking Support and Guidance: If setting boundaries is difficult, seek help from a therapist or trusted person. They can offer advice and support. For example, talking to a counsellor can give you tools to communicate your boundaries better with your friend.

Setting boundaries protects your well-being and builds healthier, more respectful relationships.

When Nita's old friend Sneha visited after many years, she saw how Nita was overwhelmed by trying to meet everyone's needs, leaving her exhausted and with no personal time. Seeing Nita's exhaustion and irritability, Sneha sat down for a heartfelt conversation. With warmth and understanding, Sneha gently pointed out the importance of setting boundaries to protect her well-being.

Sneha's words struck a chord with Nita, making her realise how crucial it was to create limits in her life. Inspired by Sneha's insight and support, Nita decided to take action. She began setting clear boundaries and carving out dedicated times for work, family, and, most importantly, herself. Nita communicated her needs and limits to those around her, learning to say no when necessary and prioritising self-care.

As Nita created space amidst the chaos, she experienced a much-needed transformation. No longer burdened by constant demands, she found renewed energy and joy. By honouring her needs and setting boundaries, Nita reclaimed control of her life and rediscovered a beautiful sense of balance. Sneha's wise advice had put her on a path of self-care and empowerment, leading her to embrace newfound freedom and fulfilment.

Women must set boundaries to prioritise their well-being, preserve their mental and emotional health, and honour their worth. Establishing limits empowers them to navigate relationships, pursue self-care, and uphold their identity, fostering resilience and authenticity in a world that often demands endless sacrifices.

Key Points
1. Establishing boundaries involves defining acceptable behaviour and interactions. This helps protect one's emotional, physical, and mental well-being and sets the tone for mutual respect and healthy relationships.
2. People-pleasers often struggle with setting boundaries. Their behaviour usually stems from deep-seated insecurities and a desire for acceptance rooted in early life experiences. It reflects a longing for belonging and self-worth by making others happy.

Setting BOUNDARIES

3. Boundaries can include personal space (e.g. requesting more distance), time (e.g. declining additional work), emotional (e.g. addressing criticism), and financial (e.g. managing loan repayments).

4. Setting boundaries starts with knowing your needs. You must set limits, communicate your needs to the people involved, and consistently reinforce them. Respecting other people's boundaries is also important.

FORGIVING AND HEALING

Shanti, a radiant 42-year-old woman with two precious children, seemed to be living the life of her dreams—a life she had longed for. Her divorce from her husband a few years ago brought her a measure of freedom, supported by substantial alimony and a successful career. Yet, beneath this mask of success lay a tumultuous past that haunted her present. Throughout her 15-year marriage, Shanti harboured a silent wish to break free from the clutches of a relationship tainted by physical, mental, and spiritual abuse inflicted by her husband. However, her attempts at liberation were constantly denied, as he held her captive in a cycle of control and manipulation.

The turning point came when Shanti faced a life-threatening episode of violence that pushed her to approach the authorities. This brave step led to a legal battle, breaking the chains of her oppressive marriage. It was the start of an arduous journey towards healing and reclaiming her freedom.

Even though Shanti was free from her troubled marriage, the pain from her past still hurt deeply. The unresolved anger and bitterness from her previous relationship cast a dark shadow over her life, making it hard for her to connect with others and see a hopeful future. Her conversations were often consumed by her ex-husband as if she were trapped in a painful loop of reliving old wounds. When she talked to her mother about her past, it felt like she was stuck on repeat, endlessly replaying her ex's wrongs. Her mother's suggestion to forgive intensified her anger and felt like a painful blow rather than helpful advice. Sharing her feelings with a friend led her to a painful realisation—her life felt like a never-ending drama, with the ghost of her past haunting every part of her. Every thought and conversation seemed tangled in the messy remnants of her old life. Overwhelmed by her past pain and unresolved issues, Shanti reached a crucial moment in her life. She began to see that her emotional burden was so heavy because she had been holding onto old hurts for too long. This new insight helped her realise that to move forward and find happiness, she needed to let go of the emotional baggage she had been carrying.

Forgiveness is often seen as a path to emotional maturity and inner peace, usually portrayed as a serene and graceful act in stories and on social media. But let's be honest—it's not as easy as it seems. Forgiving someone can feel like trying to walk a tightrope while balancing a load of bricks—it sounds impressive, but it's incredibly tough in reality. Friends and family might suggest you forgive and forget as if it's as simple as misplacing your keys, but it's not straightforward.

Forgiveness can feel like a stubborn stain on your emotional carpet: you can keep scrubbing away at it or cover it up and pretend it's not there. Sometimes, it's necessary to confront it and make a real change.

How to travel the journey of forgiveness.

1. **Acknowledge Your Emotions:** Begin by recognising and accepting the full range of your emotions, including anger, hurt, betrayal, and sadness. This step involves being honest and understanding that these emotions are valid. Shanti used this to reflect on her pain and see her ex-husband not just as a villain but as a person with his struggles.

2. **Seek Support**: Finding a trusted friend or therapist who can listen to you without judgment can bring a sense of relief. Sharing your feelings with someone who provides a compassionate and empathetic ear can be incredibly healing. Shanti found solace in her friend Leela's supportive presence, which allowed her to unload her heart and gain understanding.

3. **Practice Mindfulness**: Engage in mindfulness practices like yoga and meditation to help calm your mind and manage emotional stress. These practices can create a space for introspection and empower you to reach emotional balance. For Shanti, mindfulness became a powerful ally in reducing the emotional intensity of her pain and fostering a sense of inner peace.

4. **Set Boundaries**: Establishing boundaries in your relationships is a powerful tool to protect your emotional well-being. Boundaries help you safeguard your heart and prevent further harm as you navigate the path of forgiveness. Shanti set boundaries to ensure she didn't fall back into unhealthy patterns and to maintain her emotional health.

5. **Cultivate Gratitude**: Use gratitude as a guiding force to help you focus on positive aspects of your life. Reflect on the lessons from your experiences, the strength gained through trials, and your capacity to forgive and love. Shanti incorporated gratitude into her life as a compass, guiding her towards serenity and contentment.

6. **Seek Professional Help if Needed**: Work with a therapist or counsellor to support you through the complexities of forgiveness. Professional guidance can offer valuable tools and insights to help you navigate your emotions and move forward. Shanti's journey highlights the importance of seeking professional support to heal.

7. **Embrace the Present**: This is a crucial step in your journey towards forgiveness and emotional healing. Shifting your focus from the past to the present is vital for creating a fulfilling life. Investing your energy in current opportunities and experiences allows you to build a positive future. Shanti's story is a testament to this. She needed to create a new, hopeful life for herself and her children, focusing

on positive experiences rather than being bogged down by past hurts. Embracing the present enabled her to move forward and find joy in her current life.

8. **Embrace the Gradual Process and Allow Time for Healing**: Understand that forgiveness is a journey that unfolds gradually, not overnight. It takes time and effort. Approach it step by step, recognising that healing doesn't happen overnight. Allow yourself the space to process your emotions and gradually reduce the impact of past hurt. Each small step helps diminish the intensity of your pain, making forgiveness more manageable and effective. As you move through this journey, be patient with yourself and give time for your emotions to settle, knowing that each day brings you closer to a place of peace and healing.

9. **Forgive but Never Forget**: Embrace the concept of forgiving someone while remembering the lessons learned from the experience. Forgiveness involves letting go of resentment and anger, but it's also important to remember what happened and protect yourself from similar harm in the future. This approach allows you to move forward without carrying the weight of past grievances, promoting emotional healing and growth. It also serves as a reminder to watch out for red flags and avoid repeating past mistakes. By remembering the past with wisdom, you can approach similar situations with caution and insight.

Forgiveness is a powerful act that frees us from the weight of past hurts and grievances. It's not about excusing others but about releasing the hold of resentment on our hearts. By forgiving, we find inner peace and emotional freedom, allowing us to embrace the present with a lighter spirit. Letting go nurtures personal growth and provides love and gratitude to flourish. Forgiveness is a gift to ourselves, a vital step toward healing.

Key Points
1. By forgiving someone, we liberate ourselves. Although the path of forgiveness is difficult and long, it is worth the price for our freedom.
2. Steps forward to your forgiveness journey are:
<ul><li>Recognize and accept the full range of your feelings.</li><li>Find a trusted friend or therapist to discuss these feelings.</li><li>Shift your focus from the past to the present.</li><li>Understand that forgiveness takes time and effort.</li><li>Learn about setting boundaries</li><li>Deal with stress by engaging in mindful practices like yoga and meditation.</li><li>Let go of resentment while remembering lessons learned, to protect yourself from future harm and promote personal growth.</li></ul>

Going Back to
FAITH

My mother embodies deep religious devotion, with a faith in God that could move mountains. She always advised me to walk the same path: "If something is not in your control, leave it to God. He will take care of it." But with my endless questions and doubts, I often chose my way, sceptical of her unwavering trust.

Even in the most challenging of times, my mother remains remarkably peaceful and giving. She firmly believes that whatever you give comes back to you a hundredfold. Her calmness and generosity are a testament to her faith. As time passed, I began to see the wisdom in her words. Recently, amidst life's storms, I noticed many people remaining calm in difficult situations, all because of their steadfast belief in a higher power. They trust that every twist and turn is part of a greater plan.

While I often worry about life's uncertainties, these individuals find peace and resilience in their faith, trusting that everything happens for a reason. Their conviction is a light, illuminating the path through life's darkest valleys. In their faith, I see a refuge from the chaos, a sanctuary of peace amidst the turmoil. It's a reminder of the comfort and strength that faith offers, even in life's trials.

However, faith is not confined to religion alone. It is also found in the trust we place in the people we love, the principles we hold dear, and the potential we see in the future. Faith in humanity reflects a belief in people's goodness and potential. Despite challenges and setbacks, human beings possess fundamental decency and kindness.

Faith is a cornerstone of the human experience, offering comfort and hope in times of adversity and uncertainty. It binds us together, strengthening our communities and relationships and fostering a deep sense of belonging and mutual support. This conviction encourages us to grow, love more deeply, and cultivate virtues like patience, compassion, and humility. Faith eases our anxieties, allowing us to surrender our fears to a higher power and trust in a broader plan.

Losing faith is common during moments of deep trauma or loss when grief makes it hard to hold onto our beliefs. Whether it's the unexpected death of a loved one, long-term struggles like chronic illness or financial problems, disappointment with religious leaders, or intellectual challenges that clash with our faith, these experiences can shake us to our core. Unanswered prayers, especially in times of desperate need, and feeling unsupported by our community can leave us feeling isolated and full of doubt.

How to Rediscover Faith as a Middle-Aged Woman

1. **Quiet Introspection:** Rediscovering faith, whether religious or personal, is a journey that begins with the powerful tool of quiet introspection. This practice, which involves reflecting on your core beliefs and emerging doubts, can be immensely beneficial. After feeling disheartened by life's challenges, Anjali set aside time for personal reflection. She journaled her thoughts and feelings about her beliefs in humanity and her potential. This self-examination allowed her to confront and understand the uncertainties affecting her faith, providing a foundation for renewal.

2. **Seek Guidance:** Seeking guidance from trusted individuals can offer support and clarity as you navigate your faith journey. When Rashi faced a crisis of confidence in her career and personal life, she reached out to mentors and close friends with a positive outlook. Their supportive advice and encouragement helped her regain trust in herself and the goodness of people. Their insights provided new perspectives, reinforcing her belief in her abilities and the potential for positive change.

3. **Engage in Personal Beliefs and Values:** Reconnecting with your personal beliefs and values is

not just a step in the journey of faith rediscovery but a powerful practice that can deepen your sense of purpose and belonging. After a difficult period, Priya started revisiting the principles that had guided her life, such as her commitment to kindness and self-growth. She engaged in activities that aligned with her values, such as volunteering and personal development workshops. This reconnection helped her rediscover a sense of direction and fulfilment, reinforcing her faith in her principles.

4. **Practice Mindfulness and Reflection:** Mindfulness and reflection are essential for finding peace and grounding yourself. For instance, after experiencing stress and uncertainty, Meera began practising mindfulness and meditation regularly. These practices provided her with moments of calm and helped her reconnect with her inner self. By focusing on the present, Meera found a renewed sense of clarity and purpose, aiding her journey of rediscovery.

5. **Join a Supportive Community:** Being part of a supportive community can offer strength and a sense of belonging. After moving to a new city, Vikram joined a local group that shared his interests in personal development and community service. Engaging with this group gave him a network of like-minded individuals who supported his journey of adjustment. This connection helped Vikram feel more rooted and hopeful, reinforcing his belief in the power of collective support.

6. **Focus on Gratitude:** Practicing gratitude helps shift your perspective and recognise the positive aspects of your life. After facing several challenges, Sunita kept a gratitude journal to note daily blessings and achievements. This practice allowed her to appreciate the good in her life and find meaning in everyday moments. Sunita rediscovered a sense of wonder and connection by focusing on what she was thankful for, enhancing her overall well-being.

7. **Accept and Embrace Doubt:** Accepting and embracing doubt is crucial for personal growth and a deeper understanding of your beliefs. For instance, Smriti struggled with doubts about her potential after encountering setbacks. Instead of avoiding these feelings, she openly discussed her uncertainties with trusted advisors and explored different perspectives. This acceptance of doubt allowed Smriti to grow and develop a more resilient and nuanced understanding of her beliefs and capabilities.

Rediscovering faith is a deeply personal journey that can transform your life, offering solace and clarity amid life's uncertainties. Whether revisiting your core values, seeking guidance, or embracing mindfulness, this process helps reconnect you with a sense of purpose and inner peace. This journey helps heal past wounds and enriches your life with deeper meaning, allowing you to embrace each day with a revitalised spirit and a heart full of gratitude. Rediscovering faith is about returning to old beliefs and forging a stronger, more resilient connection with yourself and the world around you.

Key Points.
1. Faith isn't just about religion. It's also about believing in the people we love, the values we hold dear, and the possibilities we see for the future. People can have faith in many aspects of life, including their potential and the goodness in humanity.
2. Faith comforts and gives us hope in times of adversity and uncertainty. It binds us together, strengthening our communities and relationships and giving us a deep sense of belonging and support.
3. Losing faith is common during moments of deep trauma or loss when grief makes it hard to hold onto our beliefs.
4. To renew your faith, think about your beliefs and doubts. Talk to trusted friends or mentors for support and get back in touch with what you believed in before by volunteering. Practice mindfulness to calm your mind and think clearly. Join a supportive community from your faith for encouragement and connection. Keep a gratitude journal to focus on the good things in your life, and don't be afraid to explore your doubts to understand yourself better.

Finding Your
PASSION

Richa had always been a brilliant student, scoring 96 per cent in her school exams and filling her parents with pride and joy. Her path seemed inevitable, faced with the classic dilemma of choosing between medicine, engineering, or civil services. She chose medicine, the noblest of all, and enthusiastically pursued it, topping the state medical entrance examination and securing a place in a prestigious medical college. The early years of medical school were demanding, but Richa approached them with determination. Yet, beneath her diligent exterior, a quiet unease began to grow. The reality of the medical profession started to weigh heavily on her heart. It was during her internship that this unease turned into a struggle. The sight of pain, suffering, and death was almost unbearable, but Richa pushed these feelings aside, believing they were part of every medical student's journey. Her frustrations sometimes emerged as sudden outbursts, revealing the deep-seated turmoil she had long hidden.

Richa graduated with satisfactory grades, knowing

she wasn't cut out for the emotional toll of direct patient care. She chose a non-clinical speciality for her post-graduation, hoping the distance from patient interaction would bring her peace. A stable government job followed, offering comfort and sound money, but every day felt like a battle. Her job provided financial security and a semblance of purpose, but the passion and joy were missing. Years passed in a haze of routine and discontent until one fateful day, Richa decided to attend a wellness retreat. Desperate for a change and a spark of inspiration, she was introduced to the concepts of prevention and wellness. She felt a flicker of genuine interest for the first time in years. With her medical background, she dove deep into online research, spending countless hours engrossed in disease prevention.

During a heartfelt conversation with her mother, the last piece of the puzzle fell into place. Richa realised she had never been interested in curing diseases; what had always fascinated her was preventing them. This insight was life changing. With renewed determination, she began studying functional medicine. To her utter surprise, the long study hours no longer felt exhausting. She was energised and excited, genuinely enjoying the process. The joy she found in this new path was palpable, a stark contrast to the years of discontent she had experienced. After twenty years of service, Richa boldly and courageously decided to quit her secure government job. She opened her preventive treatment clinic, where she could finally do what she loved. The clinic thrived under her passionate care. Every morning, Richa woke up with a renewed sense of energy and excitement. She eagerly looked forward to seeing her patients, researching new preventative methods, and expanding her knowledge.

Her clinic became a beacon of hope for many, where prevention preceded cure. Patients left her clinic with better health and a newfound understanding of their bodies and minds. Richa had found her true passion, transforming her life and the lives of countless others.

Like Richa, you can discover your passion and feel joyful by following key steps.

1. **Acknowledge Discontent:** Start by recognising any feelings of dissatisfaction or unease in your current path. Like Richa, who felt a growing discomfort despite her success in medicine, understanding these feelings can signal that your current direction may not align with your true interests. Reflect on aspects of your life or job that leave you unfulfilled or exhausted and use this awareness as a starting point for change.

2. **Engage in Self-Reflection:** Explore your true interests and passions. Richa's turning point came when she attended a wellness retreat and discovered a genuine interest in disease prevention. Similarly, engage in activities that pique your curiosity or spark joy. This could involve hobbies, new courses, or even informal discussions with people who inspire you.

3. **Explore New Interests:** Once you identify a potential interest, dive deeper into it. Richa explored functional medicine and prevention, which aligned with her curiosity and skills. Explore ways to immerse yourself in your newfound interests through additional research, courses, or practical experiences and gauge whether the new path aligns with you.

4. **Consult with Trusted Individuals:** Seek advice from mentors, friends, or family members who understand your strengths and passions. Richa's conversation with her mother played a crucial role in clarifying her true calling. These discussions can provide valuable insights and encourage you to see your interests from different perspectives, helping you make more informed decisions.

5. **Align Skills with Passions:** Richa combined her medical knowledge with her interest in prevention to create a successful preventive treatment clinic. Similarly, assess how your abilities can be applied to areas you're passionate about. This alignment often leads to a more fulfilling and successful career or personal endeavour.

6. **Evaluate Financial Considerations:** Ensure that your pursuit of passion also considers financial stability. Richa made a significant career shift after careful consideration and planning. Balance your passion with practical financial needs to avoid frustration and ensure your chosen path supports your well-being.

7. **Take the Leap:** Once you've identified and explored your passion, be prepared to take bold steps towards it. Richa's decision to quit her secure job and open her clinic was a courageous move that allowed her to embrace her passion fully. Similarly, be willing to make changes that align with your newfound interests, even if it involves stepping out of your comfort zone.

8. **Find Joy in the Journey:** Embrace the process of pursuing your passion with enthusiasm and positivity. Richa's newfound joy in her work and her clinic's success demonstrates the fulfilment that comes from aligning your career with your passions. Approach your journey with excitement and gratitude and celebrate your progress.

Rediscovering your passion in middle age can be a decisive turning point, bringing new vitality into your daily life. It's about finding what truly excites and fulfils you, making work more than a job. Aligning your career with your passions infuses your life with renewed energy and purpose, transforming everyday tasks into joyful pursuits. This alignment enhances your satisfaction and equips you to face challenges with greater resilience. However, it's crucial to remember that turning your passion into a career should ensure financial independence, not dependence. Embracing what you love can lead to a vibrant, meaningful life where each day is driven by enthusiasm and the security of economic stability.

Key Points

To discover your passion in midlife and find joy, follow the key steps:

1. Acknowledge any dissatisfaction with your current path.

2. Explore your interests and passions by trying new activities or hobbies.

3. Research, take courses, or gain practical experience to explore potential interests further.

4. Seek advice from mentors, friends, or family who know your strengths and passions.

5. Match your skills with your passions for a fulfilling career. Ensure your pursuit of passion is financially viable.

Finding Your
PURPOSE

From a young age, Saumya's life was a testament to resilience and determination. Growing up in a lower-middle-class family, she faced a reality where basic needs often preceded education. Her family struggled to make ends meet, and the burden of financial constraints was heavy. Education, though necessary, was sometimes pushed to the background in the face of immediate needs like food and daily expenses.

Determined to pursue her dreams despite these challenges, Saumya took on various odd jobs from a young age. She worked late into the night and on weekends, doing everything from tutoring younger students to working in local shops, all to save enough money for her education. Her days were long and exhausting, filled with the pressure of balancing work and school.

The road was tough, but Saumya's resolve was unshakable. After completing her education, she secured a good job that she loved. She got married and had two kids.

Now a middle-aged woman with a comfortable job, Saumya had ample time for herself as her children had left for college. This marked the beginning of a shift in her soul. An emptiness settled in that mundane activities and superficial interactions couldn't fill. The parties and gatherings that once filled her schedule now felt hollow. Her job, once a source of passion and fulfilment, seemed like an empty routine. Saumya realised she could no longer invest time in activities or people that didn't touch her soul. She yearned to find her true calling, to understand her purpose on this earth, and to make every moment count.

Aware of the fleeting nature of time, Saumya began to treasure each passing day. No longer willing to waste her moments on superficial endeavours, she embarked on a journey of self-discovery, delving deep into her soul for answers. Through introspection and seeking inspiration, she explored various paths, each step bringing her closer to clarity.

One day, in a heartfelt moment with her house help, Saumya saw her past reflected in the struggles of her helper's bright daughter, who couldn't pursue her dreams due to financial constraints. A surge of emotion hit Saumya as memories of her own harrowing journey to education flooded her mind. In that instant, her purpose crystallised. Filled with empathy and a deep determination, she knew she had to make a difference for others facing similar challenges.

Saumya's job provided financial stability and valuable connections, giving her a platform to support a cause close to her heart: providing education to those who lacked access. Raising funds for underprivileged children became her calling—a way to fulfil her higher purpose and give back to society. She discovered a network of like-minded individuals who shared her passion and dedication. These genuine connections gave her strength and support. With each contribution towards the education of bright, underprivileged minds, Saumya felt liberated, content, and optimistic. Her life's purpose became apparent, and she embraced it wholeheartedly, radiating a contagious zest for life as she made a tangible impact on the world around her.

The bittersweet reality of middle age is when the nest is empty, and the only excitement in your career is waiting for the clock to strike five, you realise you've spent more time cooking for others than pursuing your dreams. Amid this contemplation, a spark ignites within you—a desire for something more, something beyond the mundane. Your higher purpose calls out, and hobbies that once gathered dust whisper of forgotten passions. Your soul yearns for something that ignites a fire within. With curiosity and a pinch of desperation, you embark on a quest of self-discovery. From pottery classes to extreme trampolining, you explore every avenue, turning your midlife crisis into a string of adventures. Along the way, you meet fellow travellers seeking their paths, forming a support group. But after all this, you realise it's not enough; you're searching for something more.

Finding your purpose can be a deeply fulfilling journey, much like Saumya's. Here are some steps inspired by her story to help you discover your true calling:

1. Reflect on Your Past:

Review your life and recognise the moments that shaped you. Reflect on the challenges you faced and how you overcame them. Saumya's early struggles with balancing work and education were defining moments that influenced her future path. Understanding past experiences provides valuable insights into what truly matters to you.

2. Identify What Brings You Joy:

Consider the activities that make you feel alive and fulfilled. Supporting education for underprivileged children became Saumya's source of deep joy and purpose. Identify the moments or activities that energise you and make you genuinely happy. Pinpointing these sources of joy is critical to understanding what might form the basis of your true calling.

3. Look for Patterns:

Examine these activities for common themes or patterns once you have identified what brings you joy. Saumya noticed that her passion for education and helping others was a recurring theme. Analyse the patterns to gain insight into the underlying themes that are important to you. This will help you understand how your interests and passions can be woven into a meaningful purpose.

4. Seek Inspiration:

Expose yourself to new experiences and connect with people who inspire you. Saumya's interaction with her house help's daughter, who faced financial challenges, reignited her passion and clarified her purpose. Engaging in workshops, volunteering, or conversing with people who have found their purpose can provide fresh perspectives and inspiration. These experiences can spark new ideas and help you uncover your true calling.

5. Take Action:

Start taking small but significant steps towards exploring your interests. Saumya took on various roles to save for her education and used her job's stability to support her cause. Similarly, you can begin by pursuing activities related to your interests, even small-scale ones. No matter how minor, each action will bring you closer to discovering your purpose and clarifying your true calling.

6. Build a Support Network:

Surround yourself with like-minded individuals who share your passions and values. Saumya found strength and support from a community dedicated to making a difference in education. Joining groups or communities that focus on your areas of interest can provide encouragement, motivation, and valuable connections. Engaging with others on a similar journey can offer support and new insights as you navigate your path.

7. Embrace Your Journey:

Finding your purpose is an ongoing journey rather than a destination. Saumya's purpose evolved from her life experiences and her quest for meaning. Be patient with yourself as you explore and grow. Celebrate your progress and learn from any setbacks. Embracing the journey and staying open to new experiences will help you uncover a purpose that brings you lasting fulfilment and joy.

Saumya's journey urges us to honour our emotions. It's a heartfelt reminder that the universe gently guides us toward our destined paths, but only through introspection and by embracing new encounters can we unearth our true calling. By delving into our inner selves and embracing vulnerability, we pave the way for growth.

Key Points
1. Middle age is when you get an urge to find your higher purpose. Is it because of the ample time we have or because our desires for worldly possessions have decreased? Most of us experience this change.
2. To discover your true calling in midlife, follow these steps inspired by Saumya's journey:
• Review key moments in your life and how they've shaped you.
• Pinpoint activities that make you feel fulfilled and alive.
• Analyse recurring themes in the activities you enjoy.
• Expose yourself to new experiences and connect with inspiring individuals.
• Start by taking small steps to explore your interests.
• Surround yourself with like-minded individuals who share your passions.
• Understand that finding your purpose is an ongoing process.

Part Four
Redefining Beauty

INTRODUCTION

In a world where dermatologists and plastic surgeons increasingly set the standards for beauty, the saying "beauty lies in the eye of the beholder" seems like a forgotten mantra that's faded into the background. Today, the relentless pursuit of flawlessness and eternal youth often overshadow personal self-esteem, leaving many questioning their worth and appearance. The pressure to conform to an ever-evolving ideal can be overwhelming and challenging. Now, it's time to laugh at the absurdity of these unnatural expectations and realise that the beauty industry's standards are just that unreasonable. We can redefine beauty on our terms so we embody that power!

Amid this frenzy to defy the hands of time, a glimmer of wisdom shines through the Botox haze. True beauty isn't about erasing every wrinkle or flaw but embracing the journey. After all, who needs a perfectly smooth forehead when you've got a heart full of laughter and a smile that could light up the room? As we age and grow wiser, we define beauty not only by appearance but also by health. Our well-being allows us to fully experience life, offer kindness, and contribute meaningfully to the world. The only beauty that holds any value lies in our health and how we live, reflecting a deeper, more enduring form of attractiveness that celebrates our vibrant lives.

So, here's to acceptance! Let's raise a toast to accept the changes in our bodies and wrinkles while striving to be our best version at any age. Because let's be honest, being our fabulous, imperfect selves is far more appealing than trying to squeeze into the impossible standards of our 20-year-old selves. Cheers to embracing the journey, the laugh lines, and the slightly higher weight flashing on the weighing scale. Let our journey inspire the stories our bodies tell and the wisdom we gain each year.

POT BELLIES AND ADDED KILOS

Reena stood before her wardrobe as the grand party approached, feeling disappointed. The dresses, once her favourites, were now cruel reminders of her changing body. Each garment stared back at her, highlighting her increasing inability to fit into the clothes she once wore. A wave of depression washed over her but determined to find a solution, she ventured out in search of a new dress that would make her feel fabulous, regardless of what her mirror had been insinuating lately.

Finally, she found the perfect dress that promised to transform her into the belle of the ball. A surge of happiness poured through her as she imagined entering the event, exuding confidence and allure. But when she slipped into the dress, her mind turned into a treacherous judge, pointing out each perceived flaw in merciless detail. Reena stared at her reflection, crestfallen, a deep sense of disappointment flooding her being. The dress that promised transformation now served only to accentuate every flaw. She felt vulnerable and exposed. Her confidence crumbled as she struggled to find any trace of her former self.

Instead of feeling fabulous, she was overwhelmed by the changes in her body. She blamed her hormones and faced the harsh reality, and that left her feeling more self-conscious than ever.

Desperate for reassurance, she turned to her son and husband, who were under strict orders, to offer only affirmations. "Do I look beautiful?" she nervously asked, hoping for validation. But even in their efforts to please, with forced smiles and exaggerated nods, she couldn't help but feel they were only telling her what she wanted to hear. Then, in a moment of audacious honesty, her son uttered the forbidden words, "Yes, Mommy, you have put on weight." The words hung in the air, yet they sliced through her heart. She turned away, feeling even more ashamed and demoralised.

Reena's carefree days seemed distant now, replaced by the realities of ageing that Mother Nature had brought her way. She started noticing other changes in her body beyond her control—potbelly creeping in, breasts losing firmness, skin dulling, hair thinning, and even muscle tone diminishing. The culprit? The natural decline of hormones that once defined her youthful charm.

For many women, navigating midlife brings with it a profound struggle with weight gain and body image. It's more than just clothes feeling tighter or the occasional comfort food indulgence that later leads to guilt. As menopause approaches, our bodies undergo unpredictable declines in levels of estrogen, progesterone, and testosterone. These declines reshape how we see ourselves, more often than not, because of how others see us, reminding us of time passing and the inevitability of change. They urge us to seek acceptance in a world that often prizes youth.

Interestingly, aside from humans, only a few other species experience menopause, and most female animals do not. Historically, most women didn't live long enough to experience menopause. A hundred years ago, the life expectancy for women was so low that many didn't reach menopause. However, advancements in medicine have increased life expectancy, allowing many women to experience menopause today.

Before we dig deeper, it is essential to understand some terms

Premenopause: This term refers to **the period of a woman's life before** she begins to experience the symptoms and changes associated with menopause. During premenopause, a woman has regular menstrual cycles and normal ovarian function.

Perimenopause or *Menopausal transition:* This is the **transitional phase** leading up to menopause, typically starting several years before menopause. During perimenopause, a woman's hormone levels fluctuate, causing changes in menstrual cycle regularity and symptoms such as hot flashes, night sweats, and mood swings. This stage can last for several years until menopause is reached.

Menopause: Menopause is the **point in time** when a woman has not had a menstrual period for 12 consecutive months, signifying the end of her reproductive years. This typically occurs around age 50 but can vary. It marks the cessation of ovarian function and a significant decrease in estrogen production.

Postmenopause: This refers to **the period of a woman's life after** she has reached menopause. In postmenopause, the symptoms of menopause, such as hot flashes and night sweats, often subside, but the reduced levels of estrogen may continue to affect various aspects of health. This stage continues for the rest of a woman's life.

Menopause is not a curse; it's a natural part of life. Women are born with a finite number of eggs in their ovaries. Over time, the number of eggs decreases. When the egg reserve in the ovaries diminishes significantly, perimenopausal symptoms start to appear. Menopause occurs when there are no more eggs left for ovulation.

The ovaries produce three hormones—estrogen, progesterone, and testosterone—essential for ovulation and pregnancy. Perimenopausal symptoms occur due to hormonal imbalances, and menopausal symptoms occur because these hormones decrease. During this transition, which can start years before actual menopause, women often experience weight gain, changes in body shape, and changes in skin and hair. This affects how we look.

Why does this happen? Is it because after menopause, the body no longer needs to attract the opposite sex for reproduction? This can be hard to accept, and body image becomes a significant concern. However, understanding what is happening with our bodies makes coping easier. Let us explore how hormones cause these changes and affect weight and body composition during menopause.

Estrogen: Estrogen levels decrease as women approach menopause. This hormonal shift can cause fat to be stored around the waist. You might notice weight gain around your midsection even if your diet and exercise routine haven't changed. The hormonal changes during perimenopause substantially contribute to increased abdominal obesity, which may lead to increased morbidity [1]. Additionally, lower estrogen levels can cause breasts to lose their firmness. These changes can be frustrating and disheartening, but it is a standard part of the menopausal transition.

Progesterone: Progesterone impacts mood, sleep, and water retention, which can indirectly influence weight. As progesterone levels decrease, they indirectly affect weight gain. For instance, if you are not sleeping well or are experiencing mood swings, you might find it harder to stick to a healthy diet and exercise routine. Additionally, water retention can make you feel bloated and heavier than you are.

Insulin sensitivity. Research suggests estrogen may improve glucose homeostasis by affecting various insulin-sensitive tissues and organs [2]. Estrogen improves insulin sensitivity, helping the body efficiently use insulin to control blood sugar levels. As estrogen levels decline, insulin sensitivity may decrease, making it harder to manage weight and increasing the likelihood of weight gain, particularly in the abdominal area. This decline in estrogen can contribute to insulin resistance, which is associated with obesity and various metabolic disorders. Therefore, addressing hormonal changes is crucial in managing weight and preventing metabolic complications in women

Testosterone: Studies have indicated that declining estrogen levels can increase bioavailable testosterone, which may lead to visceral fat accumulation [3].

However, after menopause, the ovaries produce less testosterone, which results in muscle loss. With less muscle, your metabolism slows down, making it harder to maintain a healthy weight. This can lead to a frustrating cycle of weight gain and difficulty losing it.

Cortisol: During midlife, cortisol levels can rise due to increased stress, which may be related to menopausal symptoms like hot flashes, insomnia, depression etc. or changes in relationships and careers. Unfortunately, higher cortisol levels can lead to more abdominal fat. Imagine feeling stressed and noticing that your belly fat increases as a result. This stress-related weight gain can compound the effects of other hormonal changes, making it even more challenging to manage your weight during menopause.

Understanding these changes can help you manage your weight and health better during menopause, which is crucial for overall well-being. While it's common to relate weight to appearance, as seen with most middle-aged women who might focus on how they look, health is the bigger concern. A healthy weight helps reduce the risk of chronic conditions such as heart disease, diabetes, and high blood pressure. As hormonal changes affect metabolism and body composition, maintaining weight supports hormonal balance and lessens joint stress, preventing pain and mobility issues. Additionally, a healthy weight boosts energy levels, combats fatigue, and allows you to stay active. It also positively impacts mental health, enhancing confidence and mood.

How to manage weight during midlife

1. Prioritise Weight Management

Maintaining a healthy weight for midlife women becomes increasingly essential due to hormonal changes, metabolic shifts, and ageing related challenges. As estrogen levels decline during menopause, women may experience weight gain, particularly around the abdominal area, compounded by slower metabolism and reduced muscle mass. Prioritising weight management involves setting clear, achievable goals and making a consistent effort to address these changes. It requires a proactive approach, including regular weight monitoring, setting realistic targets, and embracing a lifestyle that supports weight control. This might involve adopting a structured fitness routine, making mindful dietary choices, and staying informed about how hormonal changes impact weight. Regular check-ins with a healthcare provider can offer personalised advice and adjustments to strategies based on individual needs, ensuring that efforts are effective and sustainable.

2. Incorporate Regular Exercise

Regular exercise is essential for managing weight and overall health, not only during menopause and perimenopause. As women transition through these stages, hormonal changes, including decreased estrogen levels, can lead to weight gain. Regular physical activity profoundly benefits cardiometabolic, physical, and psychological health for midlife women, especially during the perimenopausal and postmenopausal years [4].

a) Resistance Training: Resistance training, also known as strength training, is crucial for middle-aged women due to its numerous benefits in combating age-related physical changes and enhancing overall health. As women enter midlife, they often experience a decline in muscle mass, bone density, and metabolic rate, partly due to hormonal changes such as decreased estrogen levels. A study found that engaging in structured resistance training two to three times a week enhanced the quality of life for postmenopausal women with vasomotor symptoms, primarily by alleviating these symptoms [5]. Vasomotor symptoms in menopausal women include hot flashes, night sweats, and flushes, which are related to changes in hormone levels that affect the body's temperature regulation and blood flow.

Benefits of Resistance Training

Preserve Muscle Mass: Women lose muscle mass with age, a condition known as sarcopenia. Strength training exercises like weight lifting, resistance band workouts, and bodyweight exercises help counteract this loss by stimulating muscle growth and strength.

Improves Bone Density: The risk of osteoporosis is a common concern for middle-aged women. Weight-bearing exercises, such as squats, lunges, and resistance band exercises, stress the bones, which helps stimulate bone formation and strengthen bone density, reducing the dangers of fractures.

Enhances Metabolic Rate: A slowed-down metabolism makes weight easier to gain and more challenging to lose. Resistance training boosts the metabolic rate by increasing muscle mass and enhancing calorie expenditure even at rest. This improves overall body composition by reducing body fat and increasing lean muscle mass.

Supports Joint Health and Functional Fitness: By strengthening the muscles around the joints, resistance training helps stabilise and protect them, reducing the risk of injuries and joint pain. Additionally, it enhances overall functional fitness, making everyday activities such as lifting, carrying, and climbing stairs easier and more manageable.

Boosts Mental Health: Resistance strength training has been shown to positively affect mental health, reducing symptoms of depression and anxiety, improving mood, and boosting self-esteem. The psychological benefits of exercise contribute to overall well-being and can enhance quality of life.

Two to three days of resistance training per week is ideal, allowing a day of rest between sessions for muscle recovery. Start with lighter weights and gradually increase the resistance as strength improves, doing 8-12 repetitions with 2-3 sets of each exercise. Focus on proper form and technique to prevent injury. Include a variety of exercises to target different muscle groups, such as squats, lunges, push-ups, rows, and shoulder presses. Incorporating various types of resistance, such as free weights, machines, and resistance bands, can provide a well-rounded workout. Work with a certified personal trainer or exercise physiologist for a personalised program to guide you in executing exercises correctly to maximise benefits and minimise injury risk.

b) Aerobic Exercise or Cardiovascular Exercise

Cardiovascular exercises like walking, jogging, cycling, and swimming efficiently manage weight during menopause. These exercises help burn calories and improve heart health. Regular exercise significantly contributes to weight loss in postmenopausal women, highlighting its effectiveness in managing menopausal weight gain. According to a study, even without weight loss, short-term regular aerobic exercise can enhance glucose and lipid metabolism in previously sedentary overweight and obese women [6].

c) Flexibility Exercises

As women age, their muscles and joints become less flexible, leading to a higher risk of injury and decreased mobility. Flexibility exercises enhance the ability of muscles and joints to move through their full range of motion. These exercises often involve stretching, which can be dynamic (movement-based) or static (holding a position). Typical forms of flexibility exercises include yoga, Pilates, and basic stretching routines.

Flexibility exercises help prevent injury from strain, maintain spine alignment for good posture, enhance mobility that eases the execution of daily tasks, and reduce stress while promoting mental well-being. Flexibility exercises should be performed at least 2-3 times a week in sessions of 10-15 minutes and include stretches for all major muscle groups.

d) Balance Exercises

These physical activities are designed to improve stability and the ability to maintain control over the body's centre of gravity. The exercises focus on strengthening the muscles that help keep you upright, including your core and legs. You can do simple activities, such as standing on one leg, to more complex movements involving stability balls, balance boards, or specific yoga and Pilates poses at least three times per week in 20-30-minute sessions.

As women age, maintaining balance becomes increasingly important to reduce the risk of falls, a leading cause of fractures and head trauma among middle-aged and older adults. These exercises can also help improve coordination and support the ability to perform daily tasks safely and effectively, such as walking, climbing stairs, and carrying objects. Strengthening the core muscles reduces the risk of back pain and other musculoskeletal issues. Balance exercises encourage concentration and mental engagement, which helps cognitive function and mental sharpness.

Types of Balance Exercises

Single-Leg Stands: Standing on one leg for a set period can significantly improve balance. Close your eyes or stand on an unstable surface to increase the difficulty.

Heel-to-Toe Walk: Walk in a straight line, placing the heel of one foot directly in front of the toes of the other foot to help improve coordination and balance.

Tai Chi: This ancient Chinese practice involves slow, deliberate movements and has been shown to improve balance and reduce the risk of falls in older adults.

Yoga: Many yoga poses, such as Tree Pose and

Warrior III, challenge balance and strengthen the core muscles.

Stability Ball Exercises: Use a stability ball for seated marches or ball squats to enhance balance and core strength.

What do the four types of exercises target?	
Resistance Training	Preserves muscle mass and improves bone density, which improves metabolism and joint health.
Aerobic Exercise	It improves cardiovascular health and reduces weight.
Flexibility Exercise	Enhances joint range of motion. Helps prevent injury from strain, maintains spine alignment for good posture, and enhances mobility.
Balance Exercise	Improves stability and coordination, which enhances the ability to perform daily tasks easily and reduces the risk of falls.

3. Recognise Lifestyle Traps and Change Your Mindset: A Simple Guide

Sedentary Habits: Many spend hours sitting in front of screens for work, entertainment, or social media. This lack of movement can lead to weight gain. Try incorporating short breaks for stretching or walking into your day to keep your body active.

Convenience Foods: Fast and processed foods might seem like a quick fix, but they often contain unhealthy ingredients that can contribute to weight gain. Instead, focus on preparing simple, home-cooked meals. Cooking at home allows you to control ingredients and portion sizes.

Reduced Physical Activity: Our busy lives can make it hard to find time for exercise, but regular physical activity is essential for maintaining a healthy weight. Look for activities you enjoy, whether dancing, gardening, or a brisk walk, and make them a regular part of your routine.

Emotional Eating: Sometimes, we eat not because we're hungry but because we're bored, stressed, or emotionally disturbed. Recognise when emotions drive your eating habits and find healthier ways to cope, like talking to a friend, journaling, or practising mindfulness.

Social Influences: Social gatherings and cultural norms sometimes encourage overeating or unhealthy food choices. Be mindful of these influences and make healthier choices even in social settings. Enjoying an occasional treat is okay, but balance it with more nutritious options.

Small Changes Lead to Big Results: Start with minor, manageable adjustments rather than overhauling your entire lifestyle at once. For instance, swap out sugary drinks for water or incorporate more vegetables into your meals. These small steps can lead to lasting changes over time.

Stay Mindful and Consistent: Awareness of your habits is the first step to change. Pay attention to how your daily choices impact your health and adjust as needed. Consistency in these small changes will build up to a healthier lifestyle.

Changing Your Mindset: Shifting your mindset can be transformative. Instead of viewing weight management as a restrictive burden, see it as a positive opportunity for growth and self-care. Embrace the journey of making healthier choices as an act of kindness to yourself. Cultivating a mindset of self-compassion and patience can help you stay motivated and resilient, even when facing challenges.

Embracing Setbacks: It's common for people to lose sight of their goals now and then, but that does not mean that they cannot get back on track and start again. Being consistent with your health goals is hard, but starting again with the same enthusiasm is harder. So next time after a holiday or if you've fallen into old patterns, have the courage to begin again, one step at a time.

By recognising these lifestyle traps and adopting a mindset that supports positive change, you can make sustainable improvements in your health and well-being. Each small step you take, combined with a compassionate and proactive attitude, will contribute to achieving and maintaining a healthier lifestyle.

Dear ladies, it's not about fitting into a dress; it's

about thriving in middle age and living our lives to the fullest. It's about embracing each day with the strength and health to pursue our dreams and fulfil our destiny. While we can't guarantee eternity, we can choose to make a meaningful impact on the world around us. Let's focus on living well, embracing our journey, and making a difference with every step.

Key Points
Menopause and Hormonal Changes: Menopause and menopausal transition are natural life stages during which hormone levels fluctuate. Estrogen levels decrease around menopause, leading to weight gain around the abdomen, reduced muscle mass, and altered skin and hair. This occurs as the ovaries' egg reserve diminishes, and hormonal imbalances affect body composition.
Impact of Hormones on Weight: Estrogen helps regulate fat distribution and insulin sensitivity, hence, decreased levels during menopause can lead to increased abdominal fat and lower metabolic rate. Progesterone and testosterone also affect mood, sleep, and muscle mass, affecting overall weight and metabolism.
Exercise Benefits: Regular exercise is crucial for managing weight and health during menopause. Resistance training preserves muscle mass and bone density, aerobic exercise improves cardiovascular health, flexibility exercises enhance joint range of motion, and balance exercises improve stability and coordination.

Lifestyle Adjustments: To manage weight effectively, recognise and address lifestyle traps such as sedentary habits, reliance on convenience foods, emotional eating, and social influences. Implementing small, manageable changes and maintaining consistency can lead to significant health improvements.

Mindset: Embracing a positive weight management and health mindset can be transformative. Instead of viewing changes as burdens, approach them as opportunities for self-care and growth. Be compassionate towards yourself, embrace setbacks, and focus on living well and thriving through middle age.

Stories On Your Face:
FINE LINES AND WRINKLES

Shreya was pleased and refreshed after her long-overdue beach vacation. In her late forties, she never cared much about her looks and lived a happy-go-lucky life. After rejoining the office, she was surprised when someone asked her what had happened to her skin. She looked closely at her reflection in the mirror for the first time in years and was taken aback to see how much her skin had changed. Fine lines, wrinkles, enlarged pores, and sunspots covered her face; she could not help but wonder what had gone wrong over the previous few years. She still exercised, ate healthily and kept herself hydrated, but she was unable to understand that menopause was knocking on her door, demanding more attention and care than she ever thought.

We often face emotional struggles that remain hidden from others through middle age. Our physical appearance, particularly our skin, becomes an evident marker of this journey. We frequently hear comments suggesting our skin's condition is due to insufficient sleep, poor diet, or inadequate skin care. However, these explanations overlook a deeper truth. The real culprit behind the changes in our skin is the natural decline of reproductive hormones. This hormonal shift is a fundamental part of ageing, influencing how our skin appears and feels. Recognise that these changes are a natural aspect of our life journey, not merely a reflection of our self-care or worth.

While we cannot directly challenge Mother Nature, we can certainly slow down the march of time. Recent research has uncovered simple tools—self-care and a healthy lifestyle—that allow us to look and feel our best even as we age. Yes, it requires effort and discipline, but the joy of feeling and looking our best surpasses all.

So, my dear middle-aged ladies, it is time to prioritise ourselves during this phase of life. Let us embrace self-care routines and indulge in healthy habits, gracefully overcoming the complexities of ageing. After all, self-care and self-love are timeless elixirs, capable of outshining any mere designation of the "haggard". Cheers to embracing the journey with grace and radiance!

While some say wrinkles are like stories on our faces, most middle-aged individuals prefer to have those tales etched in their minds rather than on their skin. But let us not despair. Instead, let's explore skin ageing, its causes, and how to prevent its signs from showing up. Think of it as a journey to maintain that youthful radiance we secretly desire.

Fine Lines and Wrinkles

Wrinkles and fine lines are natural and common signs of ageing that appear on the skin. Severalfactors contribute to the development of wrinkles and fine lines.

a) Collagen and Elastin: Collagen and elastin are proteins that play a crucial role in maintaining the health and appearance of our skin. Collagen provides strength, support, and structure to the skin, helping it stay firm and resilient. Elastin allows the skin to stretch and return to its original shape, providing elasticity.

The estrogen hormone stimulates collagen synthesis by directly influencing fibroblasts, the cells responsible for producing collagen. A decline in estrogen production reduces collagen, leading to a loss of suppleness and the development of wrinkles and fine lines.

Photoaging refers to premature skin ageing caused by prolonged exposure to ultraviolet (UV) radiation from the sun or other sources. UVA radiation is the most common type of solar UV radiation; it penetrates deeply into the skin and causes significant changes to the dermal connective tissue. According to a study, UVA radiation is responsible for the onset of photoaging and photocarcinogenesis in the early stage [7]. UV radiation can activate the enzyme matrix metalloproteinases (MMP), which increases collagen breakdown.

According to a study, smoking reduces the production

of type I and III collagens in the skin and disrupts the balance of how the skin's extracellular matrix is renewed [8]. Smoking also causes increased collagen degradation through the activation of the enzyme MMP. Smoking increases the production of free radicals and oxidative stress, leading to further collagen degradation.

Lack of sleep may lead to skin damage [9]. Sufficient sleep is essential for optimal collagen production. Lack of sleep leads to higher levels of glucocorticoids, which can damage the skin's lamellar bodies and affect skin integrity. It also disrupts the immune system, potentially harming collagen fibres. During sleep, the body undergoes repair and regeneration, including collagen production. Insufficient sleep can manifest as dull skin with reduced elasticity and increased signs of ageing. Similarly, chronic stress is also not good for the skin.

A well-balanced diet plays a vital role in collagen production. Vitamin C is essential for collagen synthesis, while the amino acids proline and glycine are the building blocks of collagen fibres. Now that we know what damages collagen, we can adopt simple practices to increase its production.

Note: Always patch-test new products if you have sensitive skin to check for any potential irritation.

Vitamin A: Vitamin A treatment decreases the expression

of matrix metalloproteinases and promotes collagen synthesis in naturally aged, sun-protected skin, similar to its effects on photoaged skin [10]. However, these creams might cause irritation and dryness; follow the instructions and talk to a dermatologist if the problem persists.

Consume vitamin A-rich foods like leafy greens, sweet potatoes, fish, etc. Vitamin A supplements are also available on the market, but exercise caution when taking them, as excessive vitamin A can have a negative effect. Do not self-medicate and take supplements without a doctor's advice.

Vitamin C: Used in anti-ageing skincare products, vitamin C creams and serums provide numerous benefits for the skin. Studies have shown that Vitamin C is a strong antioxidant for the skin. Its benefits include protecting against sun damage, reducing signs of ageing, and lightening skin discolouration [11]. Vitamin C creams are rich and moisturising, making them suitable for dry or mature skin, while serums have a lightweight texture and are great for targeting specific concerns. However, topical vitamin C is unstable; therefore, it is important to seek stable forms of vitamin C, such as ascorbic acid or sodium ascorbyl phosphate and ensure that the product is packaged in dark, opaque containers. Incorporate vitamin C into your skincare routine after cleansing and toning, and follow with a moisturiser and sunscreen in the daytime. Consistent, long-term use will yield the best results. Consult a dermatologist for personalised recommendations.

Sunscreen: The sun is one of the most common causes of collagen damage. To protect our skin from the sun, avoid prolonged exposure, especially when it is at its peak (10 AM to 4 PM). Use good quality sunscreen (above SPF 30) and reapply it after two to three hours. Wear protective clothing that covers the skin, such as wide-brimmed hats and long-sleeved shirts.

Quit Smoking: If you want to protect your collagen and want firm, supple skin, give up smoking. Various studies have shown that the skin of a forty-year-old smoker can look as old as that of a sixty-year-old.

b) Hyaluronic Acid: The moisture magnet for your skin, hyaluronic acid is like a sponge that helps to keep your skin hydrated and plump, similar to how water makes a plant look fresh and vibrant. Unfortunately, with age, our body's ability to naturally produce hyaluronic acid declines, causing the skin to lose moisture and become drier. Just like a plant without enough water starts to wilt, our skin can appear dull and wrinkled when it lacks hydration. Many studies show that hyaluronic acid-based skincare products are non-invasive and effective for boosting skin hydration and rejuvenation [12].

***c) Facial Expression*s:** Remember how your favourite T-shirt develops creases when you repeatedly fold it in the same place? The same principle applies to wrinkles caused by repetitive facial expressions. For instance, if you often frown or squint, the muscles beneath your skin create folds and lines. Over time, these lines become more prominent and visible, like the creases on a T-shirt that won't disappear even after washing.

d) Genetics: Just as your genes determine your eye or hair colour, so does it indicate your skin's predisposition to wrinkles. Some people may have inherited genes that make their skin more or less prone to wrinkling. It's like inheriting traits from your parents, such as having curly hair or a fast metabolism. While genetics play a role, lifestyle choices and skincare habits can still influence your skin's appearance and health.

To keep wrinkles and fine lines at bay, remember these simple tips:	
1. Sun Protection	Protect yourself from the sun by slathering on a broad-spectrum sunscreen with a minimum SPF of 30. Avoid direct exposure to the sun and environmental toxins.
2. Skincare Routine	Equip your skincare routine with retinol, vitamin C, and hyaluronic acid. These ingredients work together to fight ageing and dull skin.
3. Facial Expressions	Avoid repetitive expressions that deepen lines.
4. Nutritious Food	Eat wholesome food rich in vitamins A, C, and proteins.

| 5. Beauty Sleep | Get sufficient sleep to allow your skin to regenerate. |

Embrace these tips with a smile, and you'll have a fighting chance against those unwelcome signs of ageing.

Dry and Flaky Skin

As we age, our skin undergoes various changes that can result in dryness and flakiness. One factor is the reduced production of sebum, the skin's natural oil that helps to moisturise and lubricate. Additionally, the skin's protective barrier function, located in the outermost layer of the skin called the stratum corneum, becomes less effective, leading to increased water loss and decreased hydration. Moreover, the natural moisturising factors that retain water in the skin decrease over time. This disruption in the skin's moisture balance contributes to dryness and flakiness. Slower cell turnover and accumulating dead skin cells on the skin's surface further contribute to a rough and flaky texture. Environmental factors like low humidity, cold weather, and excessive sun exposure can dehydrate skin.

Adopting a skincare routine that includes gentle cleansers, hydrating moisturisers, regular exfoliation, and products containing ingredients like hyaluronic acid, ceramides, and antioxidants is essential to combat these age-related changes. Maintaining proper hydration through drinking water and avoiding prolonged exposure to harsh environmental conditions can also help alleviate dry and flaky skin.

Open Pores

With age, collagen and elastin production decreases, and the skin loses its firmness and elasticity, causing pores to appear more prominent and noticeable. The accumulation of dead skin cells can also contribute to enlarged pores by clogging them. Furthermore, sun damage and exposure to UV rays can weaken the skin's structure and lead to the breakdown of collagen and elastin, resulting in the expansion of pores. Changes in hormone levels during ageing can also affect oil production, potentially leading to clogged pores and further emphasising their appearance.

To minimise the appearance of pores, follow a consistent skincare routine, including gentle cleansing, regular exfoliation, and non-comedogenic products. Incorporating ingredients like retinol, niacinamide, and salicylic acid can help improve skin texture and reduce pore size. Protecting the skin from sun damage by using sunscreen daily is essential in preventing further enlargement of pores.

Age Spots

Age spots, also known as liver spots or solar lentigines, are flat, brown, grey, or black spots that appear on the skin due to prolonged sun exposure and ageing. They commonly develop on areas of the skin frequently exposed to the sun, such as the face, hands, shoulders, and arms. The formation of age spots is primarily attributed to the increased production of melanin, the pigment responsible for skin colour. UV radiation from the sun stimulates melanin production in certain areas, leading to the development of these spots. Additionally, the natural ageing process causes the skin to become less effective at repairing sun-induced damage, resulting in the accumulation of melanin and the appearance of age spots. Age spots are generally harmless and do not require medical treatment. However, if you are concerned about their appearance or notice any changes in size, shape, or colour, you should consult a dermatologist for further evaluation. Preventive measures, such as wearing sunscreen, seeking shade, and using protective clothing, can help reduce the risk of developing age spots.

In conclusion, remember, these skincare routines aren't just about keeping your skin looking young; they are a form of self-care, a way to honour and cherish your body as it evolves. So, embrace these practices with love and patience. After all, the goal is not to fight against time but to age with grace and confidence.

Key Points
1. Skin ageing presents as fine lines, wrinkles, dry, flaky skin, open pores, and age spots.
2. Skin ageing is primarily due to decreased reproductive hormones, but many contributory factors make the skin look aged. Sun exposure, smoking, unhealthy diet, lack of sleep, and stress are the primary contributory factors for skin ageing apart from reproductive hormones.

3. Fine lines and wrinkles primarily appear due to collagen loss. Although stopping or reversing skin ageing is impossible, we can decrease it with proper care.

4. Include the following steps to support healthy skin as you age.

- Use broad-spectrum sunscreen with at least SPF 30 to protect against sun damage and environmental toxins.
- Include retinol, vitamin C, and hyaluronic acid in your skincare routine.
- Avoid repetitive facial expressions to prevent deepening lines.
- Consume a balanced diet rich in vitamins A and C and proteins.
- Ensure adequate sleep for skin repair regularly exfoliate and cleanse to maintain a vibrant complexion.

ONCE LUSCIOUS LOCKS

A friend and I once discussed grey hair and agreed that dyeing it to cover up natural greys should be given less importance. We made a pact not to dye our hair after 50 because we wanted to age gracefully. When she turned fifty this year, I enquired about our long-forgotten promise of letting nature take its course with our hair. She was mortified by the idea and told me her heart still felt like she was in her thirties, and she could not betray her young heart by looking old.

It's true for most of us, as fifty is the new thirty. We not only feel like that but want to look young, but the tragedy is our hormones betray us as soon as we hit fifty. We need to take extra care to look how we feel, especially regarding our hair, which speaks volumes about our age compared to any other physical attributes.

Hair is a woman's crowning glory and has long been associated with our self-esteem and identity. As with time, we see them change; it's like a mirror reflecting our age. In this chapter, we will discuss the changes our hair goes through over time, and although we cannot entirely halt the process, we can slow it down with proper care. It's important to understand that although looking our best is significant, it should not come at the cost of health.

Now, let us discuss the various changes hair goes through over time.

Greying of hair

Everyone faces hair greying as a natural part of ageing. We generally get our first strand of grey in our early thirties, and by the time we reach fifty, more than half of the hair turns grey. Hair gets its colour from cells called melanocytes, which are present in hair follicles and produce the pigment that colours our tresses. However, as we age, these cells decrease in number, causing greying of hair.

Various causes of premature greying of hair

- Oxidative stress due to alcohol consumption, stress, and chronic disease
- Nutritional deficiencies like vitamin B12, vitamin D, and protein
- Drugs like antimalarial drugs
- Hypothyroidism
- Smoking
- UV rays

Much research is still being conducted to find ways to reverse or stop hair greying with age, but it is yet to be successful. However, we can still halt premature greying by addressing its root cause.

Nowadays, most urban women hide their greys by colouring or dying without considering the consequences. Although the association between hair dye use and cancer risk is still debated, more research is required in the field of hair dyes and their association with bladder cancer, childhood tumours (pregnant mothers using hair dyes), ovarian cancer and basal cell carcinoma. Some studies suggest that exposure to hair dyes may increase the risk of breast cancer [13].

Ways to minimise the harmful effects of hair dyes

- Decrease the frequency of colouring your hair.

- Do not drastically change your natural hair colour, especially lightening it, as it requires more chemicals.

- Know your product and the ingredients; basic research about them is advisable.

- Always use a known, good-quality brand.

- You can also consider using the shadow root technique, which reduces exposure to hair dye chemicals.

> **Shadow root technique of hair dying.**
>
> The shadow root technique typically keeps the roots dark while the ends are lighter, but without creating a sharp contrast between the two. Instead of a stark difference, the colourist applies dye along the length of the hair, achieving a shadow effect where the roots and the hair near them remain natural while the tips are coloured in a lighter shade. This approach results in a trendy gradient with a smooth, blurred transition between the darker roots and lighter ends. The root shadow technique is considered healthier because it reduces the frequency of colour touch-ups, minimising the amount of dye applied to the entire length of the hair. This can lead to less damage and exposure to chemicals, as the focus is on blending rather than covering the whole head. Additionally, it allows for a more natural look and can make hair maintenance easier by lessening the need for regular salon visits.

Thinning of Hair

Your heart stops when you see your falling hair, shrinking ponytail, and exposed scalp. Losing hair is a concern for women, as thick and luscious locks historically signify beauty. Generally, we attribute these changes to the hormonal shift that a middle-aged woman is experiencing, but that is just one of the culprits responsible for hair thinning during middle age. Let us discuss various causes of hair thinning:

Hormones: Estrogen deficiency can lead to increased

hair loss in women due to its role in regulating hair follicle growth. Estrogen is believed to extend the hair follicle cycle's anagen (growth) phase. When estrogen levels decrease, this growth phase may shorten, causing the hair to transition prematurely to the telogen (resting) phase. As a result, more hair enters the telogen phase, leading to increased shedding and hair loss [14].

Stress: Another major cause of hair loss and thinning in middle age is stress. Apart from the perimenopausal symptoms, stress can be because of changes in relationships, career, and appearance. A woman undergoes acute stress during this phase of their life, which causes many hair follicles to go into the resting phase, causing severe hair loss later. The good news is that as soon as the stressor is removed, the hair fall stops, and new hair grows back. Therefore, meditate, talk to a friend or therapist, or exercise to decrease stress levels.

Nutritional deficiencies: Iron, vitamin B, vitamin D, and zinc are the micronutrients required for healthy hair, and their deficiency may lead to hair loss and hair thinning. Diagnosing the deficiency is critical, as supplementation with the deficient vitamin or mineral can stop hair loss.

Damaged hair follicles: Damage to the hair follicles due to constant hair treatment and colouring can also lead to hair loss and thinning. If you see hair loss after using a product, it's advisable to stop using that product or treatment. Similarly, heat treatments can also adversely affect hair follicles and the hair shaft.

Scalp infection and inflammation: Skin diseases like psoriasis cause skin inflammation, possibly leading to hair loss.

Smoking: Studies have shown that smoking not only affects our systemic health but may lead to alopecia [15].

Sun exposure: Like skin, the hair also gets damaged by the sun, and it is called photoaging of hair. Photo damaged hair is dry with reduced strength, a rough texture, loss of colour and shine. They are also more prone to breakage

---

Ways to prevent hair thinning

- Avoid frequent hair colouring and treatment.

- Keep your scalp clean to avoid infections and inflammation. Get treatment for any scalp conditions like psoriasis.

- Eat a nutritious diet of vitamins B, D, iron, zinc, and protein. Include supplements if necessary.

- Avoid dryers and curlers to minimise heat damage.

- Avoid smoking. Protect your hair from sunlight by wearing a hat or scarf.

Treatment for thinning hair

- *Minoxidil:* **Minoxidil** is the most common topical hair treatment a doctor prescribes. It is a vasodilator that increases blood flow around hair follicles. Initially, it might cause hair loss, but the hair starts growing a few weeks into the treatment. It's essential to apply minoxidil regularly to see results. It is relatively safe and can be used for long periods.

- *Stimulating the hair follicle:* Though little research has been done, stimulating hair follicles with red light therapy and scalp massage can reduce hair loss and thinning.

- *Ayurvedic treatment:* According to Ayurveda, hair fall treatment should be holistic. It emphasises sound sleep, nutritious food, yoga, meditation, and hair massage with medicated oils three times a week. Depending on the brand, the oil can be a mixture of coconut, almond, jojoba, rosemary, argan, hibiscus, or wheat germ. Herbs such as bhringraj, brahmi, amla, neem, and shikakai support healthy hair growth and are used in oils, powders, and supplements to support hair growth. Research has shown that these oils positively affect the thickness and quality of hair. It's advisable to consult an Ayurvedic healthcare professional for personal advice.

Change in Hair Quality

Gone are the days when we flaunted effortlessly shiny, silky hair. But what causes the change in hair texture as we age? The primary cause is a decrease in our body's natural production of sebum or oils with age. Because of this, hair becomes more prone to heat and chemical damage, and requires more maintenance.

Ways to prevent change in hair quality

- Regular oiling and deep conditioning to bring back lost moisture.

- Avoid heat treatment like hot rollers and dryers.

- Avoid exposure to sun rays because sun rays damage hair. Avoid harsh chemicals, as they strip away hair moisture.

The Truth Behind Hair Care Products

How often do you expose yourself to the chemicals used in hair salons? Is it weekly, monthly or rarely? Even when sitting innocently in the salon, the air might be filled with a dangerous carcinogen, formaldehyde. Certain hair smoothening products release formaldehyde gas when heated, posing short-term and long-term health risks. Exposure to this gas may lead to respiratory problems, trigger asthma, and increase the risk of certain cancers; according to research, formaldehyde exposure may increase the risk of leukaemia [16].

Check the ingredient list for formaldehyde, methylene glycol, or formalin solution. If you are getting treated at a salon, ask whether their products contain these chemicals and what steps they can take to minimise exposure, like improving ventilation.

A study examining hair products used by Black women found that 45 chemicals linked to endocrine disruption or asthma were present, covering every targeted chemical class. The highest levels were found in cyclosiloxanes, parabens, and the fragrance ingredient diethyl phthalate (DEP), with DEP being the most common. Root stimulators, hair lotions, and relaxers often contained nonylphenols, parabens, and fragrances, while anti-frizz products were predominantly associated with cyclosiloxanes [17].

So, next time your hairdresser suggests unnecessary hair treatments, politely decline. If he recommends a cheaper product, you should be able to read the danger signs.

Ways to avoid exposure to toxins in hair products:

- Read labels.
- Reduce the frequency and amount of the hair product you apply.
- Avoid sitting in the salon if someone else is getting a hair straightening treatment, as the vapours may contain formaldehyde.
- Use products and treatments from a trusted brand.

Key Points

1. As women age, their hair undergoes natural changes such as greying, thinning, and declining hair quality.

2. Greying occurs due to decreased melanocytes, the cells responsible for hair colour. Factors like oxidative stress, nutritional deficiencies, drugs, hypothyroidism, smoking, and UV exposure can cause premature greying.

3. To reduce risks associated with hair dyes, limit the frequency of colouring, avoid drastic colour changes, research products, use high-quality brands, and consider techniques like shadow root that minimises dye contact with the scalp.

4. Hair thinning can result from hormonal changes, stress, nutritional deficiencies, damage from treatments, scalp infections, smoking, and sun exposure. Preventive measures include avoiding excessive treatments, maintaining a nutritious diet, protecting hair from the sun and quitting smoking.

5. Treatment options include minoxidil, stimulating hair follicles with red light therapy or scalp massage, and Ayurvedic treatments involving holistic practices and specific herbs.

6. Ageing reduces natural sebum production, making hair more prone to damage. Preventive measures include regular oiling, deep conditioning, and avoiding excessive heat and harsh chemicals.

7. Hair salon products may contain harmful chemicals like formaldehyde, posing health risks such as respiratory issues and cancer. Studies show that many hair products contain chemicals linked to endocrine disruption and asthma. To avoid exposure, read labels, limit product use, and choose trusted brands.

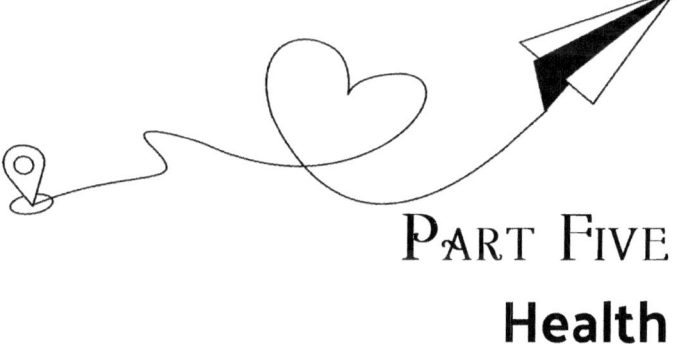

Part Five
Health

BONE AND CARDIOVASCULAR HEALTH

INTRODUCTION

When my friend Vani had surgery for the removal of the uterus and ovaries at the age of 42, she was delighted as she no longer needed to worry about trips to her doctor and monthly cycles, which were becoming shorter. After the surgery, she suddenly started noticing many changes in herself. Vani, our sleeping beauty, changed to a night owl. Someone who could not keep her eyes open after 9 pm found it hard to fall asleep, while hot flashes and insomnia disturbed her daily routine, making her irritable and moody. She didn't realise she was plagued with problems associated with a sudden decrease in reproductive hormones. She also started seeing weight gain and loss of her athletic figure, which was shocking as she was highly fitness conscious. A few years after the surgery, when she was diagnosed with osteoporosis and elevated triglyceride levels, she couldn't help but wonder what went wrong as she was the same person with the same exercise routine and eating habits.

Many women suffer in silence because they are unaware of the changes their bodies undergo with age.

Although lately, on social media, there is a lot of talk about menopausal symptoms like hot flashes, night sweats, mood swings, and depression. No one educates women about the other major changes their bodies undergo. Most women are unaware of the bone and cardiovascular changes women experience with the decline of reproductive hormones, and they do not follow some simple steps that can prevent significant diseases later on in life.

As women age, their sex hormones decline, which can lead to problems like losing bone density, rapid muscle loss, and cardiovascular diseases. Postmenopausal women are, therefore, more predisposed to fractures, knee problems, high blood pressure, cholesterol, and changes in the blood vessels. Our lifestyle should be based on the knowledge of women's changing needs with age, not just on beauty. Therefore, if you want a life in which you are independent, free of diseases, that allows you to contribute to the world, it is vital to understand the body's changing needs and act accordingly. By making informed choices, we can change our future.

BONE HEALTH

How many of us have seen our mothers and grandmothers suffering from immobility, knee problems, and spine problems, even in their fifties? Is it because of a lack of knowledge, exercise, or neglect to care for ourselves? In India, even now, self-care is a luxury, not a necessity for women. Still, if you want to live an independent, healthy life in today's era of nuclear families, you must make yourself a priority.

The silent killer of independence in older women is osteoporosis, which occurs when bones become weak and more prone to fractures. Although there can be many causes of osteoporosis, one of the primary causes in middle-aged women is a decrease in the estrogen hormone.

> **Effect of Estrogen on Bones**
>
> Estrogen regulates bone metabolism and is crucial for bone health because it influences the activity of osteoblasts, osteoclasts, and osteocytes, the cells involved in maintaining bone health. Low estrogen levels, like in menopause, affect how these cells function, producing too little new bone and increasing bone resorption. This makes bones fragile and brittle, increasing the risk of fractures.

According to research, the menopausal transition is the best time to care for bone health, and this critical period significantly impacts osteoporosis risk in older people. Bone resorption starts to rise two years before the final menstrual period, reaches its peak about a year and a half after the final menstrual period, and then levels off [1]. Therefore, women in their late forties have a few crucial years that can impact their bone health later.

Here are some ways to support your bone health during this time:

Nutrition and Supplementation for Bone Health
Calcium

Since childhood, we have seen many advertisements regarding calcium requirements for strong bones and teeth. Somehow, the notion that extensive calcium supplementation is required for strong bones has lingered in our psyche. Calcium is indeed essential for bone formation; it combines with phosphate to form hydroxyapatite, giving bones strength and rigidity. But do we require supplementation with large doses of calcium, especially in middle-aged women?

A study in postmenopausal women indicates calcium leads to a lasting decrease in bone loss and turnover, but its impact on fractures remains unclear [2]. Various studies have also shown the adverse effects of taking higher doses of calcium supplements, which may increase the risk of cardiovascular diseases like myocardial infarction [3,4]. A high consumption of **dietary calcium** seems to lower the risk of symptomatic kidney stones, while taking **calcium supplements** may raise that risk [5].

So, where to find the middle path? Women should consume 1,000–1,500 mg of calcium daily, preferably through their diet, for optimal bone health.

Some good dietary sources of calcium are:

- Milk and milk products like cheese or yoghurt
- Seeds: sesame seeds and chia seeds
- Nuts: almonds
- Vegetables and fruits: kale, broccoli, spinach and dried figs
- Food fortified with calcium like soya milk, tofu, fortified orange juice, etc.

As a middle-aged woman, your concern about getting enough calcium is legitimate. You may need to start calcium supplementation, as after menopause, women are at risk of developing osteoporosis. However, it's advisable to consult your healthcare professional, who will adjust the dose according to your requirements.

There is another catch: No matter how much calcium we consume in our diet or through supplementation, if our body is deficient in vitamin D, it will not be able to absorb calcium from the intestine, contributing to calcium deficiency.

Sun exposure is crucial for making vitamin D in our bodies as there are very few natural sources of vitamin D in our diet, like fatty fish such as salmon, tuna, mackerel, or sardines, along with mushrooms, egg yolk, and cod liver oil. People with limited sun exposure and aged individuals have greater chances of developing a vitamin D deficiency, making supplementation an excellent choice to maintain optimal vitamin D levels. Like any supplements, taking your healthcare provider's advice before starting vitamin D supplements is always good. Taking large doses of vitamin D for long periods can have drawbacks. In older women living in the community, taking high doses of cholecalciferol [Vitamin D] orally each year was associated with a higher risk of falls and fractures [6].

Exercise

When a new gym opened near our society that advertised an unbelievable body transformation in a few months, all my friends, who must be in their forties or fifties, decided to join. Some dreamt about fitting into old jeans, and some were determined to work towards their summer bodies. When this news reached me, I could not help but wonder what happened to the joint aches and pains they had been complaining about for so many months, which had become an excuse for not working out. This made me realise that women are ready to do everything in the name of beauty, but we become lazy or have hundreds of excuses if it's related to our health. I am sure I am one of them because I unknowingly worry too much about what others think of me rather than how I feel about myself.

We generally talk about going to the gym, lifting weights, and adding protein to our diet to show off our muscles, but how many middle-aged women understand the importance? Do they know about sarcopenia and decreased bone density, which plague all women as they age?

Sarcopenia is a condition primarily associated with loss of muscle mass, strength, and function. It happens with age; it can start early in one's thirties and significantly progress in older adults. It increases the risk of falls, decreases mobility, and reduces quality of life. In middle-aged women, there is the additional burden of losing bone mass with a decrease in reproductive hormones as we age.

Regaining the muscles we lose continuously and increasing bone density will help us remain mobile as the years progress. Middle-aged women, particularly those in perimenopausal and menopausal stages, need to understand their evolving needs.

Women lose a significant amount of bone density during early menopause, which may lead to osteoporosis. According to various studies, exercise training positively affects bone density in postmenopausal women [7].

Women must include the following physical exercises in their daily routine to prevent a decrease in bone density and increase muscle mass as they age.

1. *Low-impact weight-bearing exercises:* Low-impact weight-bearing exercises are physical exercises that place stress on the bones but are gentle on the joints; these are best for people who want to strengthen their bones and muscles without being harsh on the joints, for example, walking (treadmill/outside); elliptical training machines, stair-step machines and low-impact aerobics. It's advisable to avoid high-impact weight-bearing exercises like dancing, high-impact aerobics, running/jogging, jumping rope, stair climbing, and sports like tennis, basketball, volleyball, or gymnastics if you have osteoporosis or other health conditions as it increases the risk of fall and injuries. However, you can include high-impact weight-bearing exercises under the supervision of a trainer and after talking to your healthcare professional.

2. *Strength or Resistance Training:* This should include lifting weights, using elastic bands or weight machines for exercise, and using simple, functional movements such as standing or lifting one's body weight. It increases bone density and muscle mass but should be done under expert guidance.

3. *Flexibility and Balance Exercises:* Incorporating yoga and Pilates is beneficial for menopausal women to prevent falls and sprains.

An effective exercise routine for a menopausal woman may be resistance and weight-bearing exercise three days a week (on alternate days). It's advisable to rotate the training for all the muscle groups, preferably with a trainer. Brisk walking at five to six kilometres per hour, cycling, treadmill, gardening, or dancing may be done on the remaining days of the week.

Women need to understand that as life expectancy increases, it's their responsibility to take care of themselves to improve their quality of life in later years.

Key Points
1. As women age and experience a decline in sex hormones, they face increased risks of bone density loss, rapid muscle loss, and cardiovascular diseases. This makes them more susceptible to fractures, high blood pressure, high cholesterol, and atherosclerosis.
2. Menopausal women should prioritise bone health significantly, as bone density begins to decrease during this time. Weight-bearing, strength-training exercises, and proper nutrition are crucial for maintaining bone density and overall mobility.
3. Around menopause, women should aim for a daily calcium intake of 1,000–1,500 mg, mainly through their diet, and maintain optimum vitamin D levels. Sometimes, supplementation becomes essential to maintain optimum vitamin D and calcium levels. It's essential to avoid excessive supplementation and consult a doctor to tailor these recommendations to individual needs and health conditions.

CARDIOVASCULAR HEALTH

My husband always used to be jealous of me whenever our annual blood reports came in. Despite eating the same type of food and doing similar exercises, my cholesterol levels were always within the normal range while his was elevated. I never bothered much about it until I started studying the effect of female reproductive hormones on the cardiovascular system. Now, I wonder if this disparity might be due to the protective effect of my female reproductive hormones.

With so much responsibility and pressure of bearing and rearing a child, the gods seem to give us some protection by protecting our hearts during reproductive years. But jokes apart, there is a considerably lower risk of heart disease in women than men before menopause; however, after menopause, the risk of cardiovascular diseases increases in women. This is because estrogen is cardioprotective, and lower levels of estrogen are associated with cardiovascular diseases [8].

Let's discuss some common risk factors for cardiovascular diseases in menopausal women.

Central Obesity

Sometimes, I think about the close connection between beauty and health. It's amazing how our natural glow, vibrant hair, and toned physique often reflect how well we take care of ourselves. When we nurture our bodies with care, our skin radiates, our hair shines, and our figure stays fit. Yet, as we seek these ideals, it's easy to see how this balance can shift into a search for perfection through cosmetic procedures.

How many women dread the word "protruding belly," which becomes increasingly pronounced as we age? No matter how much you try to hide it, it will find a way to peek out at other people's gaze. Why is belly fat considered not a beautiful sight? Maybe because it's not healthy!

Central obesity or abdominal obesity is excess fat around the abdominal area. Unlike men, young women do not tend to accumulate fat around their abdomen but around their hips because of estrogen hormones. However, in some conditions like PCOS, where testosterone hormones increase, it may lead to central obesity in young women.

However, in middle-aged women, estrogen decreases as they approach menopause, and testosterone dominates, which is the primary contributory factor of central obesity in these women. Central obesity is linked to many diseases, like hypertension, diabetes, and dyslipidaemia. Visceral fat also accumulates around the organs, compromising their function.

The only way to deal with central obesity is to abandon your previous lifestyle. Women need to take extra care of their diet, avoid fast food, alcohol, and refined carbs, and increase their exercise to the next level because they need to cater to their bodies' evolving needs.

Hypertension

It's irony of life that, in the chaos of raising children, our blood pressure remains oddly stable despite the constant shouting and stress. We juggle endless tasks and manage households, even as our nerves fray and our patience wears thin. We tell our families we're exhausted, that our blood pressure feels on the brink, but somehow, we keep going. Yet, as the years go by, when the demands of child-rearing and job responsibilities ease and our days stretch out before us, it's as if our bodies remember all those years of strain and start to rebel. Now, with time on our hands and the energy of youth long spent, our blood pressure seems to rise, almost as if protesting the very peace that we've worked so hard to achieve. It's as if the universe has a cruel sense of timing, giving us peace only to find our bodies catching up with the toll the years have taken. Maybe it's hinting that it's your time to care for yourself.

In postmenopausal women, there is a significant

increase in blood pressure; there is no particular cause that has been identified till now, but it is attributed to various factors like central obesity, changes in the blood vessels with age, smoking, and low physical activity, apart from hormonal changes. Therefore, postmenopausal women should check their blood pressure regularly, add physical activity, quit smoking, and reduce their salt intake.

Sodium and potassium are closely related to blood pressure. We primarily get sodium from salt in our diet and processed food, which strains the blood vessels, ultimately causing high blood pressure. On the other hand, potassium promotes the excretion of excess sodium and relaxes the blood vessels, thus lowering blood pressure. The balance between sodium and potassium is essential for maintaining healthy blood pressure.

Although sodium is a vital nutrient, as it is required for the proper functioning of nerves and muscles and helps the body maintain optimum fluid balance, excess sodium is not only associated with increased blood pressure but also with the risk of kidney diseases [9].

Processed food is the primary source of sodium in our diet, Sodium can be hidden under many names in processed food, like MSG (monosodium glutamate), baking soda (sodium bicarbonate), rock salt, and Himalayan pink salt. Apart from these, any ingredient on the food label containing sodium in its name contributes to sodium in our diets. Therefore, it's essential to read and understand food labels.

Our modern diet contains too much sodium but is deficient in potassium. Evidence shows that increasing potassium reduces blood pressure and the risk of cardiovascular diseases in adults. You can include good potassium sources in your diet: bananas, avocados, potatoes, sweet potatoes, etc.

Dyslipidaemia

Cholesterol often scares us because we think of heart attacks, but it is crucial for our health. Our bodies make cholesterol to help build cell walls, aid digestion, produce vitamin D, protect nerve cells, and create important hormones. It's more than just a health worry—it's essential for many body functions. We also get cholesterol from our food in the form of saturated and trans-fats.

Cholesterol has been given a bad name because of modern lifestyles and food habits. Bad cholesterol accumulates in the arteries, leading to heart attacks. There can be various reasons for the rise in cholesterol in our bodies, and a decrease in estrogen around menopause is one of the leading causes of the increase in cholesterol in middle-aged women.

Dyslipidaemia refers to unhealthy levels of lipids (fats) in the blood. Our blood contains three types of lipids, and their levels are typically shown in your lipid profile on blood reports.

CARDIOVASCULAR HEALTH

HDL (good cholesterol)	LDL (bad cholesterol)	Triglycerides
Removes bad cholesterol (LDL) from our body.	It builds up plaque in the blood vessels, leading to heart attacks.	Triglycerides are calories you eat but don't burn right away. They are stored in fat cells and released as energy when you need them.

In postmenopausal women, there is an increase in LDL (bad cholesterol) and a decrease in HDL (good cholesterol) levels. This increase in cholesterol can lead to heart attack and stroke. Early detection is the key to avoiding complications, so it's essential to consult your doctor when your blood tests indicate dyslipidaemia so that your doctor can advise you for lifestyle changes like diet, quitting smoking, and exercise. However, if the lifestyle change and diet modification do not show desirable changes in your lipid profile, your doctor might advise you to take other measures.

So, dear ladies, as we step into this new chapter of life that offers the freedom to reconnect with friends, enjoy family dinners, and attend lively parties, we face a bittersweet reality. With time stretching, we dream of carefree days from our younger years. Yet, this freedom comes with a crucial twist: our health. Unlike before, when we could indulge without a second thought, our bodies now need more care. Our habits must be more mindful and our choices more deliberate, starting with diet and exercise.

Dietary Changes

Limit the intake of saturated fat: Common sources of saturated fats include processed meats like sausages, fatty cuts of meat, like ribs, poultry with skin, full-fat milk, and milk products. Palm oil, usually found in commercially prepared chips and *namkeen,* also falls into this category. Substitute these with good sources of saturated fats like walnuts, olive oil, and avocado.

Avoid trans-fat altogether: Trans-fats are produced industrially by hydrogenating vegetable oil, which converts liquid fat to semi-solid fat. According to the Mayo Clinic, the sources of trans-fat in our diet are commercial baked goods, such as cakes, cookies and pies, shortening; microwave popcorn; frozen pizza, refrigerated dough, such as biscuits and rolls; fried foods, including french fries, doughnuts and fried chicken, non-dairy coffee creamer and stick margarine.

It's necessary to avoid trans-fat, as it causes dyslipidaemia, which increases the risk of heart attacks, strokes, and type 2 diabetes. In India, it is tough to detect trans-fat as many of the food items sold come without any company name or food label; therefore, always buy items that come with the Food Safety and Standards Authority of India mark (FSSAI) or investigate how the food you are consuming is being prepared.

Consume foods rich in omega-3 fatty acids: Flax seeds, chia seeds, walnuts, and fatty fish, like salmon, mackerel, and sardines reduce triglycerides in the blood and improve the HDL to LDL ratio. Olive oil, avocado, and nuts may increase HDL levels in the blood.

Increase your fibre intake, especially soluble fibre. Soluble fibres form a gel-like substance in the intestine that traps cholesterol and facilitates cholesterol excretion in stool. Soluble fibre also supports gut bacteria. All fruits, vegetables, whole grains, and legumes contain some soluble fibre, but certain foods like brussels sprouts, avocados, flax seeds, and black beans contain a good amount of soluble fibre. Oats are also a good and readily available soluble fibre source, so doctors often advise eating oats if your cholesterol is high.

Exercise

Exercise is crucial for bone and heart health. Regular exercise improves the quality of life as you age. Exercise primarily improves cardiovascular health by strengthening the heart muscles, enhancing blood circulation, improving the flexibility of the blood vessels, and improving lipid profile.

As discussed before, middle-aged women's exercise routine should consist of a combination of low-to moderate-intensity aerobic exercises, resistance training flexibility, and balance exercises.

Heart Attacks During Exercise

Lately, we are hearing more and more reports of people suffering heart attacks while exercising. They seemed perfectly normal, with no health history, and some were also highly fit. So, what can be the possible cause? Yes, exercise improves heart health, but it should be done correctly. Overexertion, over speed and intensity, can strain the heart, especially in people who have led a stationary life and become suddenly active. People with underlying conditions like diabetes, hypertension, smoking history, and a family history of heart attacks need to be very careful. It's crucial to start slow and increase the intensity and duration.

A good trainer is essential if you train in the gym, one who can suggest exercises according to your target heart rate. Target heart rate is a range of beats per minute considered safe and effective for exercising. It's important because it helps you work out at a level that's good for your fitness goals, whether you're trying to lose weight, build endurance, or stay healthy. Here's why it matters:

1. *Efficiency:* Exercising within this range ensures you benefit most from your workout.

2. *Safety:* It helps you avoid overworking your heart, which can be risky.

3. *Goal Achievement:* Staying in this range can help you reach your fitness goals more effectively.

CARDIOVASCULAR HEALTH

You usually calculate a percentage of your maximum heart rate (**roughly 220 minus your age**) to find your target heart rate. For most people, the target range is about 50-85% of that maximum rate. For example, the maximum heart rate for a fifty year-old lady will be 220-50 =170, and the target heart rate will be 85 to 144 beats per minute. Besides monitoring your heart rate, watch for these signs to avoid straining your heart during exercise.

1. *Shortness of Breath:* If you're struggling to catch your breath or can't talk comfortably, you might be pushing too hard.

2. *Chest Pain or Discomfort:* Any chest pain, pressure, or tightness is a sign that you should stop and seek help.

3. *Dizziness or Light headedness:* Feeling dizzy or faint can indicate you're overexerting yourself for have a problem with your blood pressure.

4. *Unusual Fatigue:* Extreme tiredness that doesn't match your effort level could mean you're over doing it.

5. *Nausea:* Feeling sick to your stomach during or after exercise can indicate that your body is under too much stress.

6. *Unsteady Balance:* Trouble maintaining balance or coordination could be a warning that you're overexerting yourself.

Listening to your body and taking breaks can help you exercise safely and effectively. If you experience any of these signs, you must stop and consult a healthcare professional. The best age to start to look after yourself is now because prevention is always better than cure. Make your health your prime focus. Never miss your gym sessions, yoga classes, routine walks, or grocery store trips to shop for fruits, vegetables, nuts, etc. Because now, for middle-aged women, this is not a luxury but a necessity.

Key Points
1. Women's risk of cardiovascular diseases rises significantly after menopause due to the decline in estrogen, which previously provided cardiovascular protection.
2. Common risk factors for menopausal women include hypertension, dyslipidaemia, and central obesity.
3. Managing blood pressure is crucial, with a focus on balancing sodium and potassium intake. Limiting sodium and increasing potassium-rich foods can support heart health.
4. Regular exercise is essential for maintaining cardiovascular health and overall well-being.
5. Postmenopausal women often experience unfavourable changes in lipid levels, such as increased LDL (bad cholesterol) and triglycerides and decreased HDL (good cholesterol). Managing these levels through diet, including limiting saturated and trans-fats and increasing omega-3 fatty acids, is essential to reduce cardiovascular risk.

CARDIOVASCULAR HEALTH

6. Regular health check-ups, including blood pressure and lipid profiles, are essential for the early detection and management of cardiovascular diseases.

NOURISHING NUTRITION

INTRODUCTION

Every time I meet my friend Sneha, she's following the latest diet trend. Her current obsession is the keto diet, as she wants to lose weight and look her finest at her best friend's daughter's wedding. Before that, after a viral infection, she went on an anti-inflammatory diet, which she managed to stick to for only a week. Her family has given up on her and her ever-changing food preferences, and now they are reluctant to accompany her to any social gatherings or sit with her for meals.

Do you tend to follow fad diets from keto to the Mediterranean, or listen to all the YouTube health gurus to gain some insight into the elixir of youth?

Our obsession with beauty makes us follow controlled diets, and when we cannot adhere to them because of social pressure or other commitments, we start questioning our willpower. I have seen it, especially in women. We fail to understand that our aim of eating healthy should not be restricted to appearances but should focus on health. Ten years later, your external appearance will not matter, but your ability to climb the stairs will. So, let's embrace the notion that nutrition is not about fitting into your old pair of jeans but about ageing with grace and vitality.

In this chapter, we will discuss some minor changes and additions you can make to your dict to bridge the nutritional gaps and make informed food choices.

CARBOHYDRATES :
Vices and Virtues

A few weeks ago, I spoke with a middle-aged woman struggling with her weight. Six months earlier, she had shed 20 kg in three months using a strict keto diet. But now, not only had she regained those 20 kgs, she'd put on even more. The rigid keto plan had been nearly impossible to maintain, especially as a vegetarian in a country like India, where avoiding carbs is almost impossible socially. Apart from that, she was feeling depressed and was unable to focus on her work. Now, with a special event coming up, she was asking to try keto again to lose those extra kilos. Her fear of carbohydrates was palpable in her conversation, and she felt guilty about eating carbs after gaining new insight from social media about the harmful effects of carbohydrates.

I have observed that many women, especially middle-aged and teenage girls, often try various diets based on incomplete information from the internet. This may be because they are undergoing substantial emotional and physical transformations. Many women dictate their preferred diets to healthcare professionals instead of following their advice.

With our new knowledge about carbohydrate-related evils, a new fad called the keto diet emerged; the ketogenic diet is a high-fat, moderate-protein, and very low-carbohydrate eating plan. The main goal is to shift your body into ketosis, which burns fat for fuel instead of carbohydrates. The keto diet was initially developed as a therapy for epilepsy and is now used mainly to reduce weight. Although some might argue in favour of it, keto is challenging because carbohydrates are the primary fuel for our brain, and its deficiency affects mood and concentration. Your body needs time to adapt to using ketones as its primary energy source instead of glucose. This adjustment can temporarily leave you feeling low on energy, weak, or foggy. The keto diet is very restrictive; therefore, it is difficult to sustain, and long-term use can lead to nutritional deficiencies if not done under the guidance of an expert. If that's not all, social isolation is one of the primary causes of women leaving the keto diet.

My grandmother lived until she was 96. She was a hardworking lady who loved cooking meals for us. I still remember our childhood days when there was no fast food or mobile phones; we used to wait for meals prepared by her. Our plates consisted mainly of rice, roti, and millet, apart from some *dal* and *sabzi*. No one had ever heard about carbohydrates, insulin resistance, etc., but we used to be much leaner and more active than today's carbohydrate-calculating generation.

Carbohydrates are an Essential Nutrient

Carbohydrates provide the energy we need to power through the day and are essential for our brain functions. Glucose, which comes from carbs, is the primary energy source for the brain. Have you ever been grumpy when you are hungry? Do you feel starved when studying or concentrating on a project even though you are not moving much? Our brain needs a steady supply of glucose to stay happy and balanced.

Carbohydrates and Modern Diet

Before labelling carbohydrates as evil, knowing that not all carbohydrates are created equal is important. Understanding the difference helps us make informed diet choices. Carbohydrates are broadly classified into two types: simple carbohydrates and complex carbohydrates.

Simple carbohydrates provide quick bursts of energy but lack nutrients and fibre. They are often found in processed and refined foods like candy, soda, sugar, white bread, pizza, pasta, etc. They quickly get digested and cause a rapid rise in sugar levels.

Complex carbohydrates are digested slowly and gradually, releasing energy while maintaining a stable blood glucose level. They are also rich in vitamins, minerals, and fibre. They are found in whole, unprocessed foods such as fruits, vegetables, legumes, and whole grains like oats and brown rice.

Modern diets consist of large amounts of simple carbohydrates from sugary treats and refined flour and significantly less complex carbohydrates; therefore, they are rich in calories and deficient in nutrients.

Include carbohydrates in your diet judiciously.

1. Instead of simple carbohydrates, include complex carbohydrates in your diet.

2. Studies have shown that consuming nutrients like protein, fat, and fibre before carbohydrates can help reduce postprandial glucose spikes (an increase in blood glucose after meals) [10]. So, next time, start your meal with a salad bowl, followed by protein and then carbohydrates.

3. Do not choose food based on calories or carbohydrate content but on nutrition. For example, one date has more calories and carbohydrates than a teaspoon of sugar. Still, it's always good to have dates because they also contain calcium, iron, fibre, and potassium, not empty calories like sugar. If you have diabetes, be mindful of all the sources of carbohydrates in your diet, irrespective of the nutrition.

4. Avoid fruit juices, as even freshly prepared juices lack fibre and may lose nutrients during their making. Avoid packed juices loaded with sugar, preservatives, and food colouring, which hardly contain fruit juice.

Key Points
1. Carbohydrates are crucial for providing energy and supporting brain function.
2. They are categorised into simple carbohydrates, which offer quick energy but lack nutrients, and complex carbohydrates, which provide sustained energy and essential nutrients.
3. Modern diets are often high in simple carbohydrates while neglecting complex ones.
4. Include whole foods like fruits, vegetables, and whole grains to prioritise complex carbohydrates over simple ones.
5. Meal sequencing—eating protein, fat, or fibre before carbohydrates—can help manage blood glucose levels.
6. Focus on the nutritional value of carbohydrate sources rather than just their calorie or carbohydrate content.

PROTEIN POWER

When my friend joined a famous gym, she was in awe of the sculpted bodies, flat stomachs, and toned arms she saw there. She aimed for perfection all around her and went to a nutritionist to turn her dream into reality. The nutritionist inquired about her diet and informed her that her diet lacked protein, and she needed to add more than average as she wanted to build muscle mass. For the next few months, she doubled her protein, reduced her carbohydrate intake to a minimum, and started exercising regularly. When I met her after a few months, I was shocked by her physical transformation, which was brilliant. She was obsessed with how much protein and carbs she should eat; every gram of food was measured. I can't remember our conversations involving anything except discussing protein and carbs.

I believe it's good to be fit and healthy, but it should not take over all the other aspects of your life. If you are a sportsperson, a celebrity, or a trainer, it's a part of your job, and many people are involved in your fitness routine. If we try to follow the same routine with a family to look after, a time-consuming job, and no help, we are putting unnecessary pressure on ourselves to reach a beauty standard. You must do it if it's your passion, but it should not become a burden.

Protein is regarded as the ultimate superpower and is trendy in health applications, wellness circles, and celebrity diets. The traditional Indian diet lacks the optimum amount of protein and is high in carbohydrates. This can be because grains are readily available, and our ancestors required more carbohydrates as they used to do a lot of physical work.

To incorporate enough protein in our diets without worrying about it, let's discuss the functions and sources of protein so that you can make informed choices without actually fussing about it.

What are proteins and why are they important?

Proteins are essential nutrients, like construction workers, for your body. They help the body build, repair, and maintain its tissues. Protein is made up of smaller units called amino acids. There are two types of amino acids: -

Essential amino acids: Our body cannot make these amino acids independently; therefore, we must get them from our diet.

Non-essential amino acids: These are produced by the body as needed.

Middle-aged women undergo various changes

as they age, making adequate protein consumption even more critical. One significant concern for middle-aged women is sarcopenia, an age-related loss of muscle mass and function. Women must consume more protein to maintain proper muscle mass and strength. The amino acid leucine is vital for regulating muscle growth. Rich sources of leucine include whey protein, meat, fish, eggs, and soy protein isolate.

Menopausal women are at an increased risk of osteoporosis. Calcium, Vitamin D, and protein are vital in maintaining bone health. Furthermore, weight management becomes increasingly difficult for middle-aged women as metabolic rate and muscle mass decline. Protein has a satiety effect, which promotes the feeling of fullness. This helps in weight management.

Lastly, a robust immune system is essential for overall health and disease prevention, especially as women age. Protein supports the production of immune cells and antibodies that defend the body against infections and illness. By including enough protein in their diet, middle-aged women can help their immune function and overall health.

Protein Sources and Consumption

I am not in favour of calculating what goes into your mouth except to manage a disease or if you are an athlete or a trainer. A general rule of thumb for an average healthy middle-aged woman is to include a portion of a good source of protein in each meal and snack throughout the day. This ensures that your protein needs are fulfilled without actually calculating it. Factors like your level of physical activity, muscle-building aspirations, specific health objectives, or recovery from surgery may necessitate an adjustment in your protein intake. In such cases, your healthcare provider may recommend adding protein supplements to support your increased protein requirements.

Hazards of Too Much Protein

Although protein is essential, short-term high protein is sometimes required in conditions like sarcopenia, malnutrition, etc. People must understand that they should not self-prescribe protein supplements and very high-protein diets for long periods. According to various studies, a high-protein diet is associated with uric acid and calcium kidney stones, increased bone resorption, and adversely affected liver; high-protein or high-meat diets may also be linked to a greater risk of coronary heart disease because of their saturated fat and cholesterol content, and potentially even cancer [11]. Therefore, it's essential to increase your protein intake as you age, but non-judicious intake without consulting your healthcare provider can cause problems in the long run.

Good Sources of Protein

Lean poultry: This is lower in fat and cholesterol. Examples include skinless chicken breasts, turkey breasts and lean ground turkey.

Fatty fish: This is rich in protein, calcium, and Vitamin D. These are important for middle-aged women. e.g., salmon and sardines

NOTE: Eating too much fish can increase mercury in your body, which has a detrimental effect on health, especially for pregnant and lactating women. Mercury is a heavy metal that can build up in the bodies of fish. Larger and longer-lived fishes have higher levels, and eating these fish with high mercury levels also tends to increase mercury levels in our bodies. Therefore, it's advisable to have two to three servings of fish per week, choose fish with low mercury levels, like salmon and sardines, and avoid large fish with high mercury levels, like swordfish, shark, and king mackerel.

*Legumes***:** These offer plant-based proteins and are also rich in vitamins, minerals, and fibre. Examples include lentils, chickpeas, and black beans.

Nuts and seeds: Almonds, flaxseeds, and chia seeds are nutrient-dense and good sources of protein, healthy fats, fibres, and minerals.

Milk and milk products: These are significant protein sources for vegetarians as they contain all the essential amino acids and are rich sources of calcium, Vitamin D, and potassium. Yoghurt especially has the additional benefit of probiotics, which are good microorganisms found in our gut.

Key Points

1. Proteins are essential for building, repairing, and maintaining body tissues.

2. Proteins are made up of amino acids. Our body cannot produce essential amino acids that we have to get from our diet, and non-essential amino acids are the amino acids our body can produce.

3. Adequate protein intake is crucial for middle-aged women to address age-related muscle loss, osteoporosis, and weight management.

4. Include a good source of protein in each meal and snack throughout the day without obsessively counting intake.

5. Common sources include lean poultry, fatty fish (such as salmon and sardines), legumes, nuts and seeds, and dairy products. Proper intake supports muscle health, bone strength, and immune function.

6. While protein is important, excessive consumption can lead to health issues such as kidney stones, bone loss, and potential liver damage. High-meat diets may also increase the risk of certain cancers and cardiovascular diseases. Moderation and professional guidance are vital in avoiding these risks.

7. To minimise mercury exposure, choose fish with lower mercury levels, such as salmon and sardines, and limit intake of larger fish with higher mercury content, like swordfish and shark.

TABOO AROUND MILK CONSUMPTION

Milk is a significant protein source for vegetarians due to its ability to provide all nine essential amino acids the body requires. Being a complete protein source makes it a valuable addition to a vegetarian diet, helping to support various bodily functions. Additionally, milk is rich in essential nutrients such as calcium, Vitamin D, and potassium, which are crucial for overall health, particularly bone strength and immune function. Moreover, the versatility of milk allows for easy inclusion in various recipes, providing convenience in meeting protein needs.

In recent years, various concerns about milk consumption have emerged. Some health professionals advise avoiding milk altogether. Despite its nutritional benefits, milk has drawbacks.

- Lactose intolerance affects a significant portion of the population, leading to unpleasant digestive symptoms upon milk consumption, which can limit its usability as a protein source for some individuals.

- Milk allergics can trigger mild to severe reactions like hives, itching, wheezing, lips and tongue throat swelling, etc., in susceptible individuals, potentially necessitating alternative protein sources.

- The saturated fat content in whole milk and full-fat dairy products raises concerns about the impact on heart health when consumed excessively, prompting the recommendation for moderation or the selection of lower-fat options.

- Environmental considerations, including greenhouse gas emissions, water usage associated with dairy production, and ethical concerns related to animal welfare practices in the dairy industry, may influence some vegetarians' decisions to include milk in their diet.
- Nowadays, milk can have hormones given to the animals to produce more milk for commercial use, which is unsuitable for our health.

So, if you are a vegetarian with no lactose intolerance or milk allergies and you know the source of your milk, where it's coming from, and that it is free from hormones, you can include milk in your diet.

Given these factors, individuals should carefully evaluate their dietary needs, preferences, and ethical considerations when deciding whether to incorporate milk as a protein source in their vegetarian diet. Consulting with healthcare professionals or dietitians can provide personalised guidance on protein choices and ensure that nutritional goals are met effectively.

In Ayurveda, cow's milk is highly valued for its health benefits when consumed in specific ways. Warm milk spiced with cardamom, nutmeg, and cinnamon helps calm the mind and improve sleep. Cool milk with saffron and rose petals provides soothing relief for conditions like heartburn or ulcers. Golden milk with turmeric offers anti-inflammatory benefits and boosts immunity. By adjusting the temperature and adding different ingredients, milk can be tailored to address various health needs and enhance overall well-being. According to Ayurveda, milk should be consumed as a meal and preferably without any other food items in the mornings; however, it can be consumed at night before going to bed for its calming and sleep-promoting effects, but Ayurveda also tells you to avoid milk late at night because of its mucous-promoting properties and should be avoided late at night if you are prone to cough and cold.

Similarly, cow's ghee, which is clarified butter, is considered a medicine in Ayurveda that aids digestion, keeps the colon and intestinal walls healthy, is a carrier for various Ayurvedic medicines, and relieves constipation.

Curd and paneer are also considered healthy, but you need a robust digestive system to reap their benefits; therefore, for people with compromised digestive systems, it is advisable to have buttermilk and consume paneer sparingly.

VEG OR NON-VEG?

Recently, I've noticed that many women are turning to vegetarianism or even veganism due to their beliefs, personal preferences, or because they find a vegetarian diet easier on their digestive system. I was once a non-vegetarian but turned vegetarian a few years ago. Initially, it was due to a religious belief, and I gave up non-veg for a year. However, I continued with a vegetarian diet because it helped control my digestive problems. It wasn't until later that I realised I was suffering from Vitamin B12 and iron deficiencies. Before diving into this topic, I'd like to clarify the difference between vegetarian and vegan, as the terms are often confused.

Vegetarianism primarily focuses on avoiding meat for health, ethical, or environmental reasons but does not necessarily exclude other animal products like eggs, milk, and milk products.

Vegans avoid all animal products, including meat, poultry, fish, dairy, eggs, and often honey.

It's often seen in India that vegetarians and non-vegetarians constantly battle for supremacy. Non-vegetarians point out that a vegetarian diet lacks protein, while vegetarians feel proud of more nutrients and fibre in their diet and their commitment to animal welfare. So, in the clash of preferences, the age-old question remains: Which path should you take—vegetarian, non-vegetarian, or vegan? I feel it's a personal decision, and if you search the internet for supportive surveys, you will find something supporting your preference.

Our aim should be to fill the nutrient gap and follow moderation. The non-vegetarian diet lacks fibre, and the vegetarian diet lacks quality proteins, vitamin B12, and bioavailable iron.

Animal proteins are complete proteins, meaning they contain all the essential amino acids; on the other hand, plant-based proteins do not contain all the essential amino acids. You must get all the essential amino acids from various sources if you are vegan. One source might be deficient in one type of amino acid, which can be fulfilled by adding another source of protein; for example, our beloved Indian dish, *dal chawal,* is a complete protein source when combined. Lentils lack some essential amino acids that are present in rice. When consumed together, they are perfectly nutritious, ensuring the intake of all necessary amino acids. Plant proteins are less concentrated than animal proteins. Therefore, more plant food might be needed. Additionally, certain compounds in grains and legumes can block the absorption of iron and zinc.

So, if you are a vegan, to address these challenges and ensure you are getting all the essential amino acids, mix your protein sources and include a variety of plant proteins like beans, lentils, whole grains, and soy. Soy foods like tofu and tempeh should be included as they provide all essential amino acids. Soy not only postpones the physical disabilities associated with osteosarcopenia and obesity in menopausal women, but it also enhances their muscle mass and bone strength, helping to prevent the onset of osteosarcopenia [12].

Osteosarcopenia is a condition characterised by the simultaneous presence of osteoporosis and sarcopenia. Osteoporosis refers to the loss of bone density and strength, increasing the risk of fractures, while sarcopenia involves the loss of muscle mass and function. These conditions can significantly impair mobility and increase the risk of falls and fractures, particularly in older adults.

Vitamin B12 deficiency in vegans and vegetarians

As someone deeply into the world of health and wellness, I never imagined I could fall victim to a vitamin deficiency. Yet, life had other plans. A relentless stomach infection landed me in the office of a gastroenterologist, where I found myself grappling with heavy antacids for what felt like an eternity. But it wasn't just my stomach that was suffering—my spirits reached new depths, sleep eluded me, and even swallowing became a daunting task. Desperate for relief, I confided in my gastroenterologist, who, with a knowing nod, suggested checking my vitamin B12 levels. As a vegetarian with compromised eating habits due to the infection, it turned out my B12 levels had diminished, leaving me in a state of physical and emotional turmoil. But hope arrived in the form of five B12 injections. With each shot, my symptoms faded, and I was healthy and hearty in a week.

Vitamin B12, or cobalamin, is a crucial water-soluble vitamin that plays several vital roles in the body.

- It is essential for maintaining healthy nerve cells.

- It supports DNA synthesis and aids in the formation of red blood cells.
- Vitamin B12 also helps in the metabolism of fatty acids and amino acids.

Therefore, a deficiency of vitamin B12 may lead to anaemia, sleep disturbances, depression, etc.

Vitamin B12 is primarily found in animal-based foods. Meat, such as beef, lamb, pork, and poultry, like chicken and turkey, provide ample amounts of this essential nutrient. Fatty fish such as salmon and trout, as well as seafood like clams and oysters, are rich sources of vitamin B12. Dairy products, including milk, cheese, yoghurt, and eggs, significantly contribute to vitamin B12 intake. Plant-based foods do not naturally contain vitamin B12, making it challenging for vegetarians and vegans to obtain adequate levels solely through diet. This necessitates using fortified foods or supplements for those following plant-based diets to ensure sufficient vitamin B12 intake for optimal health.

For vegetarians, particularly those following a strict plant-based diet, filling the vitamin B12 gap can be achieved through several strategies. One approach is to include fortified foods in the diet, such as fortified breakfast cereals, plant-based milk alternatives (like soy, almond, and oat milk), and nutritional yeast. These fortified foods are specifically enriched with vitamin B12, providing a convenient and accessible source for vegetarians to meet their dietary needs. Another option is to incorporate vitamin B12 supplements into the daily routine. It's important to note that there can be various other causes of vitamin B12 deficiency, and being on a vegan diet is only one.

OMEGA-THREE FATTY ACIDS

I still remember my mother's stories about Bengalis and Keralites and why they are renowned for their sharp minds—apparently, it all boiled down to their love for fish. From spicy Kerala fish curry to Bengali-style macher jhol, they included fish in their staple food. Now I understand the ancient wisdom that modern social media is in a frenzy about—omega-3 fatty acids.

But what about non-coastal towns where fish was not available and, therefore, not a part of the staple diet? Now I remember my omega-3 dosages by my grandmother, who carefully crafted flaxseed mixtures with love and passed them down through generations. In North Indian households, they were known as alsi, and their benefits for brain health were touted with every spoonful. Then there were the daily chases for almonds and walnuts—it was like a game, with Mom as the enthusiastic referee, ensuring we got our daily dose of brain-boosting goodness. Now, I continue this tradition with my son, always mindful of the wisdom passed down by our elders.

So, here's to our elders, who knew about the goodness of Omega-3. Their simplicity and wisdom taught us the importance of wholesome foods long before it became a trend. Let's honour their legacy by embracing these age-old traditions and nourishing our bodies with the same love and care.

Omega-3 fatty acids are indispensable nutrients crucial for optimal health, yet our bodies cannot produce them independently, necessitating their intake through dietary sources. These essential fats exist in three primary forms: alpha-linolenic acid (ALA), predominantly found in plant-based sources like flaxseeds; eicosapentaenoic acid (EPA); and docosahexaenoic acid (DHA), prevalent in fatty fish such as salmon.

Omega-3 fatty acids, essential components of our diets, have garnered quite the reputation as nutritional powerhouses—and rightfully so. Their numerous health benefits make them a must-have in our daily nutrition.

- **Cardiovascular Benefits:** Let's start with the heart—omega-3 has been shown to have heart-health benefits, with studies indicating their ability to lower triglycerides, reduce blood pressure, and even lower the risk of heart disease and stroke. As we have already discussed, with a decline in estrogen levels, women are more prone to cardiovascular diseases.

- **Brain Health**: They're also brain boosters extraordinaire. Docosahexaenoic acid (DHA), a type of omega-3, is a major player in brain structure and function, supporting everything from cognitive development in infants to mental acuity in ageing adults, especially in post-menopausal women.

- **Anti-inflammatory:** Omega-3 anti-inflammatory powers relieve those grappling with inflammatory conditions such as arthritis, asthma, and inflammatory bowel disease.

- **Eye Health:** Once again stealing the spotlight, DHA is a crucial component of retinal tissue, making omega-3 essential for maintaining eye health. It is also beneficial for dry eye syndrome and glaucoma.

- **Depression:** Perhaps one of the most intriguing aspects of omega-3 fatty acids is their impact on depression. In a study, higher intake of dietary omega-3 fatty acids in postmenopausal women was linked to lower levels of depression in a dose-dependent way [13].

From lubricating joints to uplifting spirits, omega-3 fatty acids have rightfully earned their status as nutritional powerhouses. They are essential for overall health and can be obtained from various dietary sources.

Fatty fish: Fatty fish such as salmon, mackerel, sardines, and trout are rich in EPA and DHA, the two omega-3s most beneficial for the body.

Plant-based sources: These include flaxseeds, chia seeds, walnuts, hemp seeds, and soybeans.

Supplements: Algal oil supplements derived from algae provide a suitable alternative for vegetarians, and fish oil supplements for non-vegetarians. It is always advisable to talk to your healthcare professional if you take these supplements and stay within the recommended dose.

Omega-3 and omega-6 fatty acids are both fats that our bodies need, but they play different roles and come from other sources. Omega-6 fatty acids are also essential for our bodies, playing roles in growth, hormone production, and immune function. However, too much omega-6 can lead to inflammation because it can be converted into inflammatory compounds when consumed excessively. Our modern diet, rich in oils and processed foods, tends to be high in omega-6 fatty acids, contributing to this imbalance.

The balance between omega-3 and omega-6 in our diet is crucial. Historically, humans consumed a diet with a balanced ratio of about 1:1 or 2:1 of omega-6s to omega-3. However, today's diet has drastically shifted this ratio, with estimates suggesting ratios as high as 20:1 or even 25:1 in favour of omega-6. This shift is mainly due to the widespread use of vegetable oils in processed and fried foods and decreased consumption of omega-3-rich foods like fish and nuts.

When the ratio of omega-6 to omega-3 becomes too high, it can promote chronic inflammation linked to various diseases. To counteract this imbalance, it's essential to restore balance by increasing intake of omega-3-rich foods while moderating consumption of omega-6 from processed sources. This dietary adjustment can help reduce inflammation and support overall health.

Key Points
1. Omega-3 fatty acids are crucial nutrients our bodies cannot produce independently.
2. They must be obtained from dietary sources such as fatty fish (salmon, mackerel, sardines) and plant-based sources (flaxseeds, chia seeds, walnuts).
3. Omega-3s benefit women as they age by lowering triglycerides, reducing blood pressure, and decreasing the risk of heart disease and stroke while also supporting brain function, alleviating inflammation, and maintaining eye health. Additionally, they may help reduce depression symptoms, especially in postmenopausal women.
4. A modern diet often has an imbalance, with excessive omega-6 fatty acids (from processed foods and vegetable oils) compared to omega-3. This imbalance can lead to chronic inflammation and various health issues. To correct this, it's important to increase omega-3 intake and reduce omega-6 consumption.

FIBRE

In the warm embrace of childhood memories, I fondly recall the daily ritual of sitting down to a meal, surrounded by the rich aromas and vibrant hues of traditional Indian fare. Salad, a staple on our plates, served as a colourful invitation to embrace the wholesome goodness of vegetables. And who could forget the comforting presence of sabzi, each bite a delightful burst of flavour that awakened the senses? With a watchful eye, our mothers ensured not a single vegetable went uneaten. Now, as I play the role of the ever-persistent parent, urging my son to partake in the vegetable feast, I am met with a playful resistance fuelled by the temptations of fast food and processed treats.

While the traditional Indian diet often lacks high-quality proteins, it boasts a rich abundance of fibre, setting it apart from its protein-centric Western counterparts.

Dietary fibre is a carbohydrate in plant-based foods that our bodies can't digest or absorb. Instead, it passes through the digestive system mostly intact.

Fiber in our diet is indispensable for maintaining optimal health and well-being. It serves many essential functions in our bodies, especially for women undergoing menopausal transition and postmenopausal women. Its importance is undeniable.

Digestive Health: Fibre adds bulk to stool, facilitating its movement through the digestive tract, preventing constipation, and ensuring regular bowel movements. It also promotes gut health by serving as fuel for beneficial gut bacteria, supporting overall digestion, and lowering the risk of digestive disorders.

Heart Health: Soluble fibre binds to cholesterol in the digestive system, aiding its removal from the body. This process helps lower cholesterol levels, reducing the risk of heart disease and stroke. Oats are high in soluble fibre and, therefore, advised by healthcare professionals as a healthy addition to your heart health.

Blood Sugar Control: Fibre slows the absorption of sugar in the bloodstream, which helps regulate blood sugar levels. This is particularly beneficial for managing diabetes and reducing the risk of developing high blood sugar.

Weight Management: High-fibre foods are more filling, which helps curb appetite and reduces overall calorie intake, thereby supporting effective weight management.

It's important to add a good source of fibre to all your meals; here are some good sources of fibre-rich food.

Whole Grains: Oats, quinoa, and brown rice provide a hearty source of fibre.

*Fruits***:** Especially those consumed with their skin, offer juicy sweetness and fibre.

Vegetables: Broccoli, spinach, kale, and other vibrant vegetables deliver a crunchy, fibre-packed punch.

Legumes: Beans, lentils, and chickpeas offer fibre and protein in every savoury bite.

Nuts and Seeds: Nuts and seeds add a satisfying crunch and can be enjoyed sprinkled over yoghurt or baked into granola.

Incorporating these fibre-rich foods into daily meals satisfies taste buds and provides essential nutrients for optimal health and vitality.

In today's fast-paced world, the average diet often needs to meet the recommended fibre intake despite its crucial role in maintaining optimal health. Traditional sources of fibre have been gradually replaced by convenience foods and processed snacks that are often low in fibre and high in refined sugars and fats. This shift towards a more Westernised diet has contributed to this deficiency in fibre intake. These modern dietary habits prioritise convenience over nutrition, leading to a decline in the consumption of whole, fibre-rich foods. As a result, many individuals are missing out on fibre's numerous health benefits.

GUT MICROBIOME AND PROBIOTICS

After ten days of antibiotic treatment for my stomach infection, Vitamin B12 injections for deficiency, and a short course of probiotics, I was still not feeling the same. I was tired, depressed, and moody, with no pain but indigestion issues like bloating. After much research, I concluded that it was because of the change and decrease in good gut bacteria caused by antibiotic treatment, and it would take effort and time to restore it. I included various types of natural probiotics in my diet apart from taking probiotic supplements; it took me around six months to return to my usual self.

Many of us hate taking antibiotics and try to avoid them as much as possible because of the unpleasant symptoms associated with them. But many times, it becomes essential to take antibiotics to fight infections. Some people experience bloating, gas, diarrhoea, and sometimes prolonged treatment with antibiotics can affect our mood and immunity. Have you ever wondered why? This is because antibiotics adversely affect our gut microbiome.

Trillions of microorganisms live inside our large intestine, called the gut microbiome. The gut microbiome mainly consists of bacteria found in the coecum. Let us discuss its essential functions.

1. It helps digest complex molecules in our food, especially vegetables and meat. Imbalances in

the gut microbiome (dysbiosis) may play a role in the pathophysiology of IBS (irritable bowel syndrome), and many treatment plans for IBS are based on balancing the gut microbiome.

2. A healthy microbiome is connected with a healthy immune system; imbalances may be associated with weak immune system or autoimmune disorders.

3. The gut microbiome affects the central nervous system, and various studies have shown that it significantly affects mood, stress response, and other brain functions.

4. It protects the integrity of the gut's mucosa and inhibits harmful microbes' growth.

5. It metabolises essential nutrients and provides enzymes necessary for synthesising nutrients like vitamins K, B1, B9, and B12.

Dysbiosis

Gut dysbiosis is an unhealthy microbiome caused by the loss of beneficial microbes, overgrowth of harmful microbes, or loss of microbial diversity. Typical symptoms of gut dysbiosis are gas, bloated stomach, poor digestion, lower abdominal pain, diarrhoea, or constipation.

There can be many causes of dysbiosis, such as

- A diet rich in refined carbohydrates and deficient in fruits and vegetables.
- Antibiotics treatment.
- Stress.
- Intestinal parasites.
- Acute or chronic infections.

To manage dysbiosis:

- Limit your intake of refined, processed food and increase your intake of fruits and vegetables rich in prebiotic fibre, which feeds the good bacteria.
- Your doctor might prescribe medicines if the dysbiosis is due to harmful microbes.
- Antibiotics kill the beneficial bacteria. Therefore, dysbiosis after antibiotic consumption can be treated with probiotics supplements.
- Include probiotic food like yoghurt, pickles, and sauerkraut in your diet to increase good bacteria in your gut.

Probiotics: Probiotics are live microorganisms that, when consumed, benefit our body. Probiotics for gut health can come either in the form of supplements or food sources like yoghurt, pickles, and sauerkraut.

Key Points

1. The gut microbiome is the microorganism present in the coecum of the large intestine. It helps in digestion, increases the availability of vitamin B and vitamin K, maintains the integrity of the gut, and affects immunity and brain functions.

2. Include natural probiotics in your daily diet to help maintain a healthy microbiome. It is present in yoghurt, pickles, and kombucha sauerkraut.

3. Antibiotic treatment can kill healthy bacteria in our intestines and may lead to dysbiosis, causing symptoms like bloating, gas, constipation, and diarrhoea; therefore, it is advisable to have probiotic supplements during and after antibiotic treatment.

ADDICTIONS TO DE-ADDICTION
Navigating Alcohol

Growing up in Indian society, I've always been a teetotaller, but my inner feminist couldn't help but raise a glass to challenge the age-old taboo surrounding women and alcohol. I found myself in spirited debates, defending women's right to enjoy a drink just like their male counterparts. Yet, as I delved deeper into health and wellness, I couldn't ignore the truth: our ancestors may have had a point. While my feminist spirit may have been ready to break down barriers, my newfound knowledge shed light on the unique hazard alcohol poses for women.

Alcohol affects women differently than men due to several physiological differences, including body composition and metabolism. Women's bodies have higher fat, which retains alcohol, and lower water content, which dilutes alcohol more than men's; therefore, when women consume alcohol, their bodies tend to absorb it more quickly, leading to higher blood alcohol levels compared to men of the same weight. Additionally, women have lower levels of an enzyme that breaks down alcohol in the stomach, further contributing to increased blood alcohol concentrations. It is said that one drink for a woman equals two drinks for a man.

Alcohol can have several adverse effects on women's health, particularly as they age. Women face a higher risk of developing end-stage liver disease from alcohol use compared to men. Research indicates that women are more prone to liver injury even after consuming less alcohol [14].

Alcohol may disrupt hormone levels in women, particularly estrogen, playing a crucial role in reproductive function [15].

Many studies have supported that alcohol promotes depression [16]. One of the most common mental health issues associated with alcohol consumption in females is depression. Alcohol is a central nervous system depressant, and prolonged use can disrupt the brain's natural balance of neurotransmitters, leading to depressive symptoms such as sadness, hopelessness, and loss of interest in activities. Women are particularly vulnerable to alcohol-related depression, as they tend to experience higher rates of mood disorders compared to men.

Anxiety disorders are another common mental health concern among females who consume alcohol excessively. While alcohol may initially produce feelings of relaxation and stress relief, it can exacerbate anxiety symptoms over time. Chronic alcohol abuse can disrupt the brain's stress response system, leading to heightened anxiety levels and increased susceptibility to panic attacks and other anxiety disorders.

Additionally, alcohol can impair cognitive function and decision-making abilities, particularly in females. Excessive alcohol consumption can interfere with memory and concentration, making it difficult to perform daily tasks and meet responsibilities. Long-term alcohol abuse may also lead to cognitive decline and dementia in older women.

According to various research, excessive alcohol can negatively impact sleep quality [17]. Lack of sleep exacerbates existing mental health problems or contributes to the development of new ones. Disrupted sleep patterns due to alcohol use can increase the risk of mood disturbances, cognitive impairment, and overall psychological distress.

Many studies highlight how alcohol consumption is linked to an increased risk of breast cancer in women [18]. Even moderate alcohol intake has been associated with a higher risk of developing breast cancer, making it advisable for middle-aged women to limit their alcohol consumption to reduce this risk.

Research indicates that alcohol consumption adversely impacts puberty in females, disrupts regular menstrual cycles and reproductive function, and alters hormone levels in postmenopausal women [19].

These effects of alcohol use can also have significant consequences for bone health.

Moderate alcohol consumption, when limited to one standard drink, may have social and psychological benefits, such as stress reduction and social bonding. On the other hand, binge drinking, which involves consuming a large amount of alcohol in a short period, poses significant health risks. It is associated with a higher risk of accidents, injuries, alcohol poisoning, liver disease, and other adverse health outcomes. Women are particularly vulnerable to the harmful effects of binge drinking due to physiological differences such as lower body weight and differences in alcohol metabolism compared to men. Moreover, binge drinking on weekends or occasional heavy drinking episodes can lead to a range of short-term and long-term health consequences, including impaired judgment, memory loss, blackouts, addiction, and mental health issues. Overall, while moderate alcohol consumption may have some potential risks, binge drinking poses significant dangers and should be avoided.

Safe Drinking Habits for Women:

- Limit alcohol consumption to no more than 14 grams per day.
- Avoid drinking on an empty stomach; always eat meals when drinking.

- Refrain from drinking daily.
- If an alcohol use disorder is identified, seek appropriate counselling and pharmacologic therapy.

Navigating social situations where alcohol is prevalent can be like walking a tightrope, balancing between enjoying the moment and staying true to our health goals. It's tempting to join in the festivities, clinking glasses and toasting to life's moments with champagne in hand. But as we raise our glasses, we must remember that our health should always take centre stage. While it's perfectly okay to indulge sometimes in moderate alcohol consumption, we must be mindful not to let social pressures or expectations lead us down a path of excess. So, let's raise a glass to moderation and savour the moments without losing sight of our well-being. After all, laughter and good company are the best ingredients for a memorable celebration, even without the champagne flowing freely. Cheers to finding the perfect balance between socialising and self-care!

Key Points
1. Women have higher body fat and lower water content than men, leading to quicker alcohol absorption and higher blood alcohol levels. Women also have lower levels of the enzyme that breaks down alcohol, increasing blood alcohol concentrations.

2. Women are at higher risk of developing end-stage liver disease compared to men from the same consumption of alcohol.

3. Alcohol can affect estrogen levels, impacting bone health and reproductive function.

4. Excessive alcohol may impair memory concentration, increase the risk of breast cancer and depression, and reduce the quality of sleep.

5. Women should limit alcohol consumption to 14 grams per day. Avoid drinking on an empty stomach; always eat meals when drinking. However, it's always best to avoid alcohol altogether.

Highs and Lows of
CAFFEINE

I *belong to the foothills of the Himalayas, where even the Indian summers have a mild chill in the air. My ancestors found warmth in a simple ritual: tea for the soul. For the men, it was the alcohol to ward off the cold, while the women found solace in the comforting spices of masala chai, a potion to keep the chill at bay. Though decades have passed since they departed from those frosty lands, the tradition remained in our family. If a shiver sends a chill down your spine, tea is the remedy; if joy fills your heart, tea is the celebration; if sorrow clouds the skies, tea is the comforting embrace. And even as the night descends, tea is the faithful companion, soothing the weary soul.*

Now, fate has its ways. I am married to a South Indian whose love for tea matches mine. It could be the memories of colder climates from our childhoods, where the warmth of tea was a constant comfort. Yet, life holds surprises, and in the warm embrace of our new home, our son has forged his love affair—with iced tea. Oh, the irony of it all!

In this chapter, I will scrutinise my tea, even though it has been my best companion from childhood to adulthood.

Caffeine is a natural stimulant in various plants, such as coffee beans, tea leaves, and cacao pods. It belongs to a class of compounds known as methylxanthines. Caffeine acts on the central nervous system, temporarily promoting wakefulness and alertness. It achieves this by blocking the action of adenosine, a neurotransmitter responsible for promoting sleep and relaxation. Additionally, caffeine can enhance the release of neurotransmitters such as dopamine and norepinephrine, which can further increase alertness and improve mood. Caffeine is commonly consumed in vitamin beverages like coffee, tea, energy drinks, soft drinks, and certain medications and supplements.

Caffeine addiction, or caffeine dependence, happens because caffeine affects our brains and bodies in specific ways. Consuming caffeine blocks the calming effects of adenosine in the brain by acting on adenosine receptors. Caffeine bears a striking resemblance to adenosine, a neurotransmitter present in our brains. Both molecules share the trait of being soluble in both water and fat, enabling them to penetrate the blood-brain barrier effortlessly. Adenosine acts as a safeguard within the brain, slowing down nerve cell activity. However, owing to its structural likeness, caffeine competes for adenosine receptors. Consequently, caffeine hinders adenosine's ability to decelerate nerve activity and accelerates nerve activity. This results in heightened stimulation, increased alertness, a surge of energy, and, occasionally, the onset of coffee jitters.

Caffeine can also boost the activity of dopamine, a neurotransmitter linked to pleasure and reward, in the brain's reward pathways. This can make us feel good and can lead to a desire to consume more caffeine. Using caffeine regularly can cause changes in the brain, such as adjusting the number of adenosine receptors and altering how other neurotransmitters are released. These changes can result in developing tolerance to caffeine and experiencing withdrawal symptoms when caffeine intake is reduced or stopped.

While that morning cup of coffee or tea may offer a much-needed boost to start the day, middle-aged women must cautiously approach caffeine consumption. The hormonal shifts that accompany perimenopause and menopause can significantly heighten sensitivity to caffeine's effects, potentially amplifying its impact on health. Some potential ill effects of caffeine in middle-aged women include:

Menopausal Symptoms: Caffeine intake has been positively associated with vasomotor symptoms [20]. Therefore, reduce caffeine consumption if you suffer from vasomotor symptoms like hot flashes and night sweats.

Sleep Disturbances: Middle-aged women may already experience changes in sleep patterns due to hormonal fluctuations. Caffeine consumption negatively affects various aspects of sleep, including total sleep time, how quickly one falls asleep, time spent awake after initially falling asleep, sleep efficiency, and overall sleep structure. The extent of reduced total sleep time is influenced by both the amount of caffeine consumed and how close to bedtime it is ingested. In particular, larger doses taken nearer to bedtime lead to a more significant decrease in total sleep duration [21].

Anxiety: Caffeine consumption can negatively impact and may increase the risk of developing anxiety [22]. Excessive caffeine consumption can exacerbate these symptoms of anxiety.

Generally, moderate caffeine intake is considered safe, and black coffee is deemed beneficial to cardiovascular health. Middle-aged women need to be mindful of their caffeine intake and consider reducing consumption if they are experiencing hot flashes, night sweats, anxiety, and sleep problems.

The humble cup of tea, or coffee is a beloved companion through the highs and lows of life. But let's not forget that behind that comforting brew lies a potent stimulant; caffeine is the world's most widely consumed drug. Yes, you heard that right—our morning pick-me-up is essentially a legal dose of energy in a cup! I'm not saying we need to bid farewell to our cherished rituals entirely, but perhaps it's time to shift our perspective. Think of caffeine not as a daily necessity but as a delightful indulgence, a luxurious treat to savour rather than a habitual crutch. After all, there's something undeniably decadent about sipping on that perfectly brewed beverage, knowing it's a rare delight rather than a mundane routine. So, let's raise our mugs to moderation and imbibe in the spirit of enjoyment rather than necessity.

Key Points
1. Caffeine is a natural stimulant in coffee beans, tea leaves, and cacao pods.
2. It increases wakefulness and alertness by blocking adenosine, a sleep-promoting neurotransmitter.
3. It enhances the release of dopamine and norepinephrine, improving mood and alertness.
4. Caffeine can exacerbate vasomotor menopausal symptoms like hot flashes and night sweats; consider reducing intake if experiencing these symptoms.
5. It may worsen sleep issues due to hormonal changes; avoid caffeine later in the day.
6. Excessive consumption of caffeine can increase anxiety.
7. Be mindful of caffeine's effects on menopause symptoms, sleep, and anxiety. Enjoy caffeine in moderation as a delightful indulgence, not a routine crutch.

SMOKING AWAY LIFE

Abha grew up in a conservative Indian society where smoking and alcohol were strictly forbidden. However, when she joined a prestigious college, the desire to fit in drove her to smoke for the first time, marking the beginning of her dependence. What started as occasional puffs quickly turned into a heavy reliance on smoking, significantly, as the pressures of education intensified, and alcohol became less accessible on the campus during afternoons. Now in her forties, Abha looks much older, grappling with various health issues that stem from years of addiction. Despite her attempts to quit, the stress of her high-pressure job always leads her back to the comfort of a cigarette. Married but without children, Abha has never faced the dilemma of setting an example for kids.

I think in today's modern world, all of us know the big warning that comes with cigarette advertisements or cigarette packets that cigarette smoking is injurious to health, but still, why do so many people smoke? Have you ever seen people consuming anything with a warning it's injurious to health except cigarettes and alcohol? Another question remains: if it's so dangerous, why are governments not banning it like cocaine?

Like Abha, most people start smoking under peer pressure, and one puff leads to another. A cigarette typically contains 10 to 12 gm of nicotine. And Nicotine is addictive. Once the nicotine enters the bloodstream with each puff, it reaches our brain and rewards it with feel-good dopamine. Slowly, we have an easy way of dealing with all the unpleasant feelings in our lives, that is smoking, but the irony is it doesn't stop here; soon, you require more and more nicotine to get rid of the same unpleasant feelings like anxiety, stress, anger etc., and you become dependent on it, and even if you want to let go of it, withdrawal symptoms bring you back to your old habit.

We have so many habits, but why is cigarette smoking considered a significant health risk, especially for middle-aged women? Tobacco use exposes individuals to a dangerous mix of thousands of toxic chemicals, many of which are known carcinogens. During middle age, women deal with lots of changes due to a decrease in reproductive hormones, like changes in the skin, cardiovascular changes, and changes in bone, apart from exaggerating these changes, cigarette smoking significantly increases the risk of certain types of cancers.

Skin: Smoking causes premature ageing and wrinkles. "Smoker's face" displays distinct features, including noticeable wrinkles, pronounced underlying bone structure, and a greyish, thinning complexion [23].

Cardiovascular Health: You may have heard about cases where many fit and young individuals experience heart attacks. You might wonder why this happens despite the person exercising regularly and maintaining a good diet. Upon closer examination, these cases are often linked to a history of heavy smoking. Smoking harms overall health and cardiovascular systems [24]. Smoking affects cardiovascular health in many ways

1. Nicotine in cigarettes leads to high blood pressure.
2. Smoking increases inflammation, which may cause plaque build-up in the arteries.
3. Smoking cigarettes increases heartbeat and is also linked to cardiac fibrosis.
4. Cigarette smoking thickens the blood and may form clots in blood vessels, leading to coronary artery diseases, heart attacks and stroke.

Bone Health: Cigarette smoking is an independent risk factor for osteoporosis. Middle-aged women, especially around menopause, are prone to osteoporosis because of a decrease in estrogen and smoking further aids in these changes, putting a middle-aged woman who smokes in greater danger of developing osteoporosis.

Apart from that, we are all well aware of the increase in the risk of developing lung cancer and lung diseases in smokers, but the risk is higher in women compared to men. For women who smoke, the likelihood of dying from heart disease or lung cancer is greater than the risk of dying from breast cancer starting at age 40 [25]. Therefore, it's more important for middle age women to quit smoking.

It's easier said than done, but the best way to lead a healthy life is to quit smoking. In reality, quitting smoking is a journey that people often struggle with as they attempt to stop smoking. For Abha, her journey began when she started suffering breathlessness following a simple activity, and her X-ray showed changes in her lungs due to smoking, which made her realise every breath was the price she had to pay for the pleasure of a puff. It was an expensive trade-off that she was not ready to do now. Here's how Abha successfully quit smoking:

1. **Set a Quit Date:** Abha chose a specific date to quit smoking. This decision helped her mentally and physically prepare for the change, making the process more manageable.

2. **Identify Triggers:** She took the time to identify the situations, emotions, and routines that triggered her urge to smoke. By understanding these triggers, she developed strategies to avoid or handle them effectively. Her primary triggers were social gatherings and office pressure. She took a month off from her office and avoided all the social gatherings where alcohol was served and smoking was prevalent.

3. **Seek Support:** Abha informed her friends, family, and colleagues of her decision to quit. Their

encouragement provided her with the motivation and accountability she needed.

4. **Use Nicotine Replacement Therapy (NRT):** To ease withdrawal symptoms and cravings, Abha used nicotine patches and gum, which helped her gradually reduce her nicotine dependence.

5. **Consider Prescription Medications:** Abha consulted her healthcare provider about medications such as varenicline and bupropion (Zyban). These medications supported her in managing cravings and reducing the urge to smoke.

6. **Practice Stress Management:** Stress is a major trigger for smoking. She engaged in activities that helped reduce stress, such as exercise, meditation, and hobbies. This approach enabled her to manage cravings and prevent relapse.

7. **Stay Active:** Just like nicotine in cigarettes triggers a pleasure response by stimulating dopamine release, exercise releases feel-good chemicals called endorphins. Regular physical activity became a crucial part of Abha's routine. It helped her improve her mood, manage potential weight gain, and reduce stress, which were common concerns when quitting.

8. **Celebrate Milestones:** Abha rewarded herself for reaching significant milestones, such as one week, one month, and eventually one year without smoking. She celebrated her one-year smoke-quitting anniversary by taking an expen-

sive holiday to France with her husband. This time, she was able to save some money for the holiday because she had quit her expensive habit of smoking. These celebrations kept her motivated and reinforced her commitment to staying smoke-free.

9. **Get Professional Help:** Whenever she faced challenges, Abha sought support from a counsellor who specialised in smoking cessation. This professional guidance provided additional strategies and support to help her stay on track.

Through these steps, Abha was able to overcome her addiction to smoking and improve her health, proving that with determination and the right strategies, quitting smoking is achievable. Now, after a year, Abha feels much better. Her X-ray showed positive changes, and her lung health is much better. She looks and feels much younger.

Passive Smoking

In India, smoking is not very prevalent among women. Especially if you have kids at home, but smoking is still very prevalent among men. Some women get so used to having someone around them who smokes that they do not get bothered by cigarette smoke. Passive smoking is strongly linked to a higher risk of various diseases and health issues, particularly in children [26]. So, it would help if you avoided it.

How you can avoid environmental cigarette smoke:

Create and Choose a Smoke-Free Environment: Establish a strict no-smoking policy in your home and car. Make sure all family members and visitors understand and respect this rule. Opt for restaurants, parks, and other public areas designated as smoke-free. Many cities have laws that prohibit smoking in specific public spaces.

Communicate with Smokers: If you know someone who smokes, have an open conversation about your concerns. Ask them to refrain from smoking around you or in enclosed spaces. Support friends or family members who are trying to quit smoking. Share resources and information about smoking cessation programs.

Use Air Purifiers: Consider using air purifiers with HEPA filters to help reduce airborne smoke particles in your home, especially if you live with a smoker.

Always remember smoking is not only injurious to your health but also to the health of your loved ones.

Key Points

1. Smoking is addictive due to nicotine, which stimulates the brain's release of dopamine, creating pleasurable feelings. As dependence grows, individuals require more nicotine to cope with negative emotions, leading to withdrawal symptoms when attempting to quit.

2. Smoking significantly increases health risks for middle-aged women, including a higher likelihood of cancers. It also accelerates skin ageing and contributes to cardiovascular issues and osteoporosis due to hormonal changes.

3. To quit smoking, set a specific quit date and identify triggers while seeking support from friends and family. Utilising nicotine replacement therapy, exercise, meditation and consulting healthcare providers can help manage cravings and make the quitting process more manageable.

4. Passive smoking raises the risk of diseases. Creating a smoke-free environment and using air purifiers can help reduce exposure to harmful smoke.

Conclusion

Writing this book has been more than just a project; it has been a deeply healing journey. Throughout this process, I have experienced personal growth and change. I hope my insights and research on middle-aged women can offer guidance to those seeking answers to questions often overlooked in our daily lives.

As we move from youth to old age, with middle age in between, it's important to truly engage with and appreciate this stage of life, full of its unique challenges—whether difficult, joyful, or complicated. This book will be a supportive companion as you navigate and shape your experiences in life.

References

PART FOUR: Redefining Beauty

1. Davis, S. R., Castelo-Branco, C., Chedraui, P., Lumsden, M. A., Nappi, R. E., Shah, D., & Villaseca, P. (2012). I understand weight gain at menopause. *Climacteric, 15*(5), 419–429. https://doi.org/10.3109/13697137.2012.694066
2. De Paoli, M., Zakharia, A., & Werstuck, G. H. (2021). The role of estrogen in insulin resistance: A review of clinical and preclinical data. *The American Journal of Pathology, 191*(9), 1490–1498. https://doi.org/10.1016/j.ajpath.2021.06.006
3. Janssen, I., Powell, L. H., Kazlauskaite, R., & Dugan, S. A. (2010). Testosterone and visceral fat in midlife women: The Study of Women's Health Across the Nation (SWAN) fat patterning study. *Obesity (Silver Spring), 18*(3), 604–610. https://doi.org/10.1038/oby.2009.251
4. Hulteen, R. M., Marlatt, K. L., Allerton, T. D., & Lovre, D. (2023). Detrimental changes in health during menopause: The role of physical activity. *International Journal of Sports Medicine, 44*(6), 389–396. https://doi.org/10.1055/a-2003-9406
5. Berin, E., Hammar, M., Lindblom, H., Lindh-Åstrand, L., & Spetz Holm, A. C. (2022). Effects of resistance training on quality of life in postmenopausal women with vasomotor symptoms. *Climacteric, 25*(3), 264–270. https://doi.org/10.1080/13697137.2021.1941849
6. Wiklund, P., Alen, M., Munukka, E., Cheng, S. M., Yu, B., Pekkala, S., & Cheng, S. (2014). Metabolic response to 6-week aerobic exercise training and dieting in previously

sedentary overweight and obese pre-menopausal women: A randomized trial. *Journal of Sport and Health Science, 3*(3), 252–258. https://doi.org/10.1016/j.jshs.2014.02.002

7. Battie, C., Jitsukawa, S., Bernerd, F., Del Bino, S., Marionnet, C., & Verschoore, M. (2014). New insights in photoaging, UVA-induced damage and skin types. *Experimental Dermatology, 23*(Suppl 1), 7–12. https://doi.org/10.1111/exd.12388

8. Knuutinen, A., Kokkonen, N., Risteli, J., Vähäkangas, K., Kallioinen, M., Salo, T., Sorsa, T., & Oikarinen, A. (2002). Smoking affects collagen synthesis and extracellular matrix turnover in human skin. *British Journal of Dermatology, 146*(4), 588–594. https://doi.org/10.1046/j.1365-2133.2002.04694.x

9. Kahan, V., Andersen, M. L., Tomimori, J., & Tufik, S. (2010). Can poor sleep affect skin integrity? *Medical Hypotheses, 75*(6), 535–537. https://doi.org/10.1016/j.mehy.2010.07.018

10. Varani, J., Warner, R. L., Gharaee-Kermani, M., Phan, S. H., Kang, S., Chung, J. H., Wang, Z. Q., Datta, S. C., Fisher, G. J., & Voorhees, J. J. (2000). Vitamin A antagonizes decreased cell growth and elevated collagen-degrading matrix metalloproteinases and stimulates collagen accumulation in naturally aged human skin. *Journal of Investigative Dermatology, 114*(3), 480–486. https://doi.org/10.1046/j.1523-1747.2000.00902.x

11. Al-Niaimi, F., & Chiang, N. Y. Z. (2017). Topical vitamin C and the skin: Mechanisms of action and clinical applications. *Journal of Clinical and Aesthetic Dermatology, 10*(7), 14–17.

12. Bravo, B., Correia, P., Gonçalves Junior, J. E., Sant'Anna, B., & Kerob, D. (2022). Benefits of topical hyaluronic acid for skin quality and signs of skin aging: From literature review to clinical evidence. *Dermatology Therapy, 35*(12), e15903. https://doi.org/10.1111/dth.15903

13. Gera, R., Mokbel, R., Igor, I., & Mokbel, K. (2018). Does the use of hair dyes increase the risk of developing breast cancer? A meta-analysis and review of the literature. *Anticancer Research, 38*(2), 707–716. https://doi.org/10.21873/anticanres.12276

14. Mirmirani, P. (2016). Hormones and clocks: Do they disrupt the locks? Fluctuating estrogen levels during menopausal transition may influence clock genes and trigger chronic telogen effluvium. *Dermatology Online Journal, 22*(5), 13030/qt32r353c4.
15. Babadjouni, L. U. S. C., Pouldar, F. D., Hedayati, B., Evron, E., & Mesinkovska, N. (2021). The effects of smoking on hair health: A systematic review. *Skin Appendage Disorders, 7*(4), 251–264. https://doi.org/10.1159/000512865
16. Kang, D. S., Kim, H. S., Jung, J. H., Lee, C. M., Ahn, Y. S., & Seo, Y. R. (2021). Formaldehyde exposure and leukemia risk: A comprehensive review and network-based toxicogenomic approach. *Genes and Environment, 43*(1), 13. https://doi.org/10.1186/s41021-021-00183-5
17. Helm, J. S., Nishioka, M., Brody, J. G., Rudel, R. A., & Dodson, R. E. (2018). Measurement of endocrine disrupting and asthma-associated chemicals in hair products used by Black women. *Environmental Research, 165*, 448–458. https://doi.org/10.1016/j.envres.2018.03.030

PART FIVE: Health and Nutrition

1. Karlamangla, A. S., Burnett-Bowie, S. M., & Crandall, C. J. (2018). Bone health during the menopause transition and beyond. *Obstetrics and Gynecology Clinics of North America, 45*(4), 695–708. https://doi.org/10.1016/j.ogc.2018.07.012
2. Reid, I. R., Mason, B., Horne, A., Ames, R., Reid, H. E., Bava, U., Bolland, M. J., & Gamble, G. D. (2006). Randomized controlled trial of calcium in healthy older women. *The American Journal of Medicine, 119*(9), 777–785. https://doi.org/10.1016/j.amjmed.2006.02.038
3. Bolland, M. J., Avenell, A., Baron, J. A., Grey, A., MacLennan, G. S., Gamble, G. D., & Reid, I. R. (2010). Effect of calcium supplements on risk of myocardial infarction and cardiovascular events: Meta-analysis. *BMJ, 341*, c3691. https://doi.org/10.1136/bmj.c3691

4. Li, K., Kaaks, R., Linseisen, J., & Rohrmann, S. (2012). Associations of dietary calcium intake and calcium supplementation with myocardial infarction and stroke risk and overall cardiovascular mortality in the Heidelberg cohort of the European Prospective Investigation into Cancer and Nutrition study (EPIC-Heidelberg). *Heart, 98*(12), 920–925. https://doi.org/10.1136/heartjnl-2011-301345
5. Curhan, G. C., Willett, W. C., Speizer, F. E., Spiegelman, D., & Stampfer, M. J. (1997). Comparison of dietary calcium with supplemental calcium and other nutrients as factors affecting the risk for kidney stones in women. *Annals of Internal Medicine, 126*(7), 497–504. https://doi.org/10.7326/0003-4819-126-7-199704010-00001
6. Sanders, K. M., Stuart, A. L., Williamson, E. J., Simpson, J. A., Kotowicz, M. A., Young, D., & Nicholson, G. C. (2010). Annual high-dose oral vitamin D and falls and fractures in older women: A randomized controlled trial. *JAMA, 303*(18), 1815–1822. https://doi.org/10.1001/jama.2010.594
7. Hejazi, K., Askari, R., & Hofmeister, M. (2022). Effects of physical exercise on bone mineral density in older postmenopausal women: A systematic review and meta-analysis of randomized controlled trials. *Archives of Osteoporosis, 17*(1), 102. https://doi.org/10.1007/s11657-022-01140-7
8. Xiang, D., Liu, Y., Zhou, S., Zhou, E., & Wang, Y. (2021). Protective effects of estrogen on cardiovascular disease mediated by oxidative stress. *Oxidative Medicine and Cellular Longevity, 2021*, 5523516. https://doi.org/10.1155/2021/5523516
9. Malta, D., Petersen, K. S., Johnson, C., Trieu, K., Rae, S., Jefferson, K., Santos, J. A., Wong, M. M. Y., Raj, T. S., Webster, J., Campbell, N. R. C., & Arcand, J. (2018). High sodium intake increases blood pressure and risk of kidney disease. From the Science of Salt: A regularly updated systematic review of salt and health outcomes (August 2016 to March 2017). *Journal of Clinical Hypertension, 20*(12), 1654–1665. https://doi.org/10.1111/jch.13408
10. Kubota, S., Liu, Y., Iizuka, K., Kuwata, H., Seino, Y., & Yabe, D. (2020). A review of recent findings on meal sequence: An

attractive dietary approach to prevention and management of type 2 diabetes. *Nutrients, 12*(9), 2502. https://doi.org/10.3390/nu12092502

11. Delimaris, I. (2013). Adverse effects associated with protein intake above the recommended dietary allowance for adults. *ISRN Nutrition, 2013*, 126929. https://doi.org/10.5402/2013/126929
12. Tang, S., Du, Y., Oh, C., & No, J. (2020). Effects of soy foods in postmenopausal women: A focus on osteosarcopenia and obesity. *Journal of Obesity and Metabolic Syndrome, 29*(3), 180–187. https://doi.org/10.7570/jomes20006
13. Chae, M., & Park, K. (2021). Association between dietary omega-3 fatty acid intake and depression in postmenopausal women. *Nutrition Research and Practice, 15*(4), 468–478. https://doi.org/10.4162/nrp.2021.15.4.468
14. Maddur, H., & Shah, V. H. (2020). Alcohol and liver function in women. *Alcohol Research, 40*(2), 10. https://doi.org/10.35946/arcr.v40.2.10
15. Handy, A. B., Greenfield, S. F., & Payne, L. A. (2024). Estrogen and alcohol use in women: A targeted literature review. *Archives of Women's Mental Health*. https://doi.org/10.1007/s00737-024-01483-9
16. Awaworyi Churchill, S., & Farrell, L. (2017). Alcohol and depression: Evidence from the 2014 Health Survey for England. *Drug and Alcohol Dependence, 180*, 86–92. https://doi.org/10.1016/j.drugalcdep.2017.08.022
17. Helaakoski, V., Kaprio, J., Hublin, C., Ollila, H. M., & Latvala, A. (2022). Alcohol use and poor sleep quality: A longitudinal twin study across 36 years. *Sleep Advances, 3*(1), zpac023. https://doi.org/10.1093/sleepadvances/zpac023
18. Smith-Warner, S. A., Spiegelman, D., Yaun, S. S., et al. (1998). Alcohol and breast cancer in women: A pooled analysis of cohort studies. *JAMA, 279*(7), 535–540. https://doi.org/10.1001/jama.279.7.535
19. Emanuele, M. A., Wezeman, F., & Emanuele, N. V. (2002). Alcohol's effects on female reproductive function. *Alcohol Research & Health, 26*(4), 274–281.

20. Faubion, S. S., Sood, R., Thielen, J. M., & Shuster, L. T. (2015). Caffeine and menopausal symptoms: What is the association? *Menopause, 22*(2), 155–158. https://doi.org/10.1097/GME.0000000000000301
21. Gardiner, C., Weakley, J., Burke, L. M., et al. (2023). The effect of caffeine on subsequent sleep: A systematic review and meta-analysis. *Sleep Medicine Reviews, 69*, 101764. https://doi.org/10.1016/j.smrv.2023.101764
22. Liu, C., Wang, L., Zhang, C., et al. (2024). Caffeine intake and anxiety: A meta-analysis. *Frontiers in Psychology, 15*, 1270246. https://doi.org/10.3389/fpsyg.2024.1270246
23. Ortiz, A., & Grando, S. A. (2012). Smoking and the skin. *International Journal of Dermatology, 51*(3), 250–262. https://doi.org/10.1111/j.1365-4632.2011.05205.x
24. Parmar, M. P., Kaur, M., Bhavanam, S., et al. (2023). A systematic review of the effects of smoking on the cardiovascular system and general health. *Cureus, 15*(4), e38073. https://doi.org/10.7759/cureus.38073
25. Woloshin, S., Schwartz, L. M., & Welch, H. G. (2008). The risk of death by age, sex, and smoking status in the United States: Putting health risks in context. *Journal of the National Cancer Institute, 100*(12), 845–853. https://doi.org/10.1093/jnci/djn140
26. Cao, S., Yang, C., Gan, Y., & Lu, Z. (2015). The health effects of passive smoking: An overview of systematic reviews based on observational epidemiological evidence. *PLOS ONE, 10*(10), e0139907. https://doi.org/10.1371/journal.pone.0139907

Printed in Great Britain
by Amazon